"Dance with me," Kit whispered

Only then did Monica hear from the stage "Blue Christmas"—a slow smoky version meant for snuggling close. She opened her mouth to say no, but her lips wouldn't form the word. Her body was too busy screaming yes. And in the wake of her indecision, he took her hand and led her to the dance floor.

He held her gently at her waist, heat resonating from his palms and tingling down to her toes. He kept at a respectable distance, giving the appearance of a polite dance between associates. But there was nothing polite about the hunger in his gaze or the way it made her feel. That was Grade-A carnal, and as they rocked to the music, a giddy dizziness came over her.

"Spend the night with me," he uttered quietly. "Come with me tonight and let me wake up with you in the morning."

Immediately, desire waged war with her reason. This was wrong in so many ways. The man was a client, and though there was no corporate policy against dating one, it broke every personal rule she had.

"I've got a number of things we didn't get to Monday night." Then he bent close and murmured a sampling, making her change her *no* to a big fat *yes*.

Blaze

Dear Reader,

It was nearly three years ago when I read the very first Harlequin Blaze Encounters, Leslie Kelly's *One Wild Wedding Night* (a great story and highly recommended by this author!). My first impression was what a fun concept it was—several short stories all intersecting during one special evening. My very next thought was that an office Christmas party would be another ideal setting for such a concept.

Fortunately, my editors agreed.

I've worked in an office for almost thirty years now and have been to more corporate functions than I can count. So this was especially fun for me to spend some time imagining what might have been going on under our noses while we were busy grazing the buffet tables.

I hope you enjoy reading this story as much as I enjoyed writing it. Please drop me a note and tell me what you think of it at www.LoriBorrill.com.

Happy reading!

Lori Borrill

Lori Borrill

ONE WINTER'S NIGHT

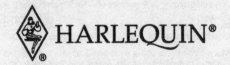

HARLEQUIN®

TORONTO • NEW YORK • LONDON
AMSTERDAM • PARIS • SYDNEY • HAMBURG
STOCKHOLM • ATHENS • TOKYO • MILAN • MADRID
PRAGUE • WARSAW • BUDAPEST • AUCKLAND

Recycling programs
for this product may
not exist in your area.

ISBN-13: 978-0-373-79581-9

ONE WINTER'S NIGHT

www.eHarlequin.com

Printed in U.S.A.

ABOUT THE AUTHOR

An Oregon native, Lori Borrill moved to the Bay Area just out of high school and has been a transplanted Californian ever since. Her weekdays are spent at the insurance company where she's been employed for more than twenty years, and she credits her writing career to the unending help and support she receives from her husband and real-life hero. When not sitting in front of a computer, she can usually be found at the baseball field, playing proud parent to their son. She'd love to hear from readers and can be reached through her website at www.LoriBorrill.com.

Books by Lori Borrill

HARLEQUIN BLAZE

308—PRIVATE CONFESSIONS
344—UNDERNEATH IT ALL*
392—PUTTING IT TO THE TEST
430—UNLEASHED
484—THE PERSONAL TOUCH
548—INDISCRETIONS

*Million Dollar Secrets

Prologue

"THERE'S EXCITEMENT in the air. Can you feel it?"

Jeannie Carmichael grinned as she surveyed the ballroom she'd spent all day transforming from a sterile beige shell into a festive holiday wonderland.

And she'd done a spectacular job of it, if she didn't mind saying.

"I mean, I know it's just an office Christmas party, but—" she shrugged and took a quick sip of her orange soda "—I don't know. The night feels electric somehow."

Her coworker Troy Hutchins followed her gaze across the large room as he swallowed down the last of a sweet-and-sour meatball. "Sure. I know what you mean," he said, though Jeannie suspected he was only humoring her. Troy tended to be agreeable that way.

In truth, she was probably just suffering from a giddy combination of nerves and anticipation. She'd spent weeks arranging this party single-handedly and on a budget slashed in half from the year before. She'd had to get creative with the food and decorations in order to afford the two things everyone insisted were vital: an open bar and entertainment. When Stryker & Associates cut staff in Operations this year, the task of organizing the annual party fell on Jeannie's plate—as most jobs with no logical home did. Being her first time at it, she'd wanted to make a good impression, and with the purse strings tightened, she'd feared the drop in amenities would end up reflecting poorly on her.

It had been tough to pull off, but so far so good. As she tapped her foot to a perky version of "Here Comes Santa Claus," she noted that people were laughing and gobbling the food. From the portable stage, Gordy Goodnite, the disc jockey she'd rented, spun plenty of Christmas swing while trying to coax couples onto the dance floor. And Jeannie was certain after another round of drinks, plenty of them would oblige. For the time being, only Hank Ascona shuffled at the edge of the stage while chatting with some of his fellow brokers.

She eyed two people from Accounting pointing to the glittery snowflakes Jeannie had hung from the ceiling. It had been a good idea to dim the lights over the dance floor. It seemed to make them sparkle more, almost as if they were giving off a glimmer all their own.

As she sat at a table and scanned the room, it looked as though everyone was having a good time. Dinner conversations were focused on Leonora's homemade lumpia and the steamed pork buns from Alan Chan's family bakery, two treats that took the edge off the fact that the food was potluck this year in lieu of the usual caterer. Jeannie had fretted over it all for weeks, and now felt rather silly for losing so much sleep.

This whole night was going off without a hitch, a fact that tickled her pink. And…well…something really *was* in the air tonight, adding a special sizzle that mixed with the beat and mingled with the crowd.

"Where'd you get the Santa Claus?" Troy asked.

She glanced back toward the windows where a man in a

red tailored suit chatted casually with their CFO, Monica Newell. Though the suit wasn't the classic fur-trimmed ensemble, and he'd traded in the shiny boots for polished black oxfords, there was no mistaking the man for St. Nick. He had the cherry-red cheeks and snow-white beard, a bag of presents tossed over one shoulder and a candy cane in his hand.

And if that wasn't enough, he simply looked...jolly.

The man was definitely brought in to spread some cheer, though by whom, she had no idea. He wasn't in Jeannie's budget that was for sure.

"I didn't," she said, watching the man converse with their executive.

Gordy Goodnite had eaten up all she'd allotted for entertainment, and even if she'd had enough left over to rent a Santa, she couldn't have gotten someone as pricey-looking as the man standing across the room. She'd seen the standard rental agency hires, and Kris Kringle over there wasn't one of them. He'd cost someone some serious money, but so far she hadn't been able to think of who. Whenever she'd spotted the man, by the time she'd made her way through the crowd, he'd disappeared. It was almost eerie the way he could be there one minute, then suddenly vanish like snowflakes on asphalt the next.

"I've got no idea what he's doing here," she added. But certainly before the evening was over, she intended to find out. Though she hadn't seen him so much as sneak a cookie, she knew he was either a party crasher or someone's special guest. If he was the former, she'd get rid of him. And if he was the latter, she'd like to know who to thank for the unexpected help.

Troy shrugged it off and went back to his plate. "Stryker probably hired him."

"That doesn't seem likely. If he wanted a Santa he would

have had me arrange it. It's strange." She picked up a carrot stick and nibbled it absently. "He's not an employee. That beard is most definitely for real. But I can't see who would have hired him. Do you think maybe he's related to someone?"

"Why don't you go over and ask him?"

Jeannie made a face. "Not while he's talking to Monica. That woman scares me."

"Monica Newell?"

"Yes. I only go near her when I absolutely have to."

Troy scoffed. "She's just a little stiff. She's not that bad."

"*Not that bad?* You heard she wouldn't let anyone in Finance wear shorts to the company picnic. She said it wasn't professional and wouldn't be tolerated as long as she was in charge."

Troy smiled and nodded. "Yeah, I heard that."

"And then Mr. Stryker himself shows up in cargo shorts."

Troy chuckled as she studied the woman, standing straight as a soldier, not a hair out of place in her cream-colored wool slacks and red turtleneck sweater. The outfit was exactly Monica—festive but perfectly understated without a solitary adornment that might be mistaken for frivolity. Or fun. In Jeannie's opinion, the ensemble would have been much improved with a colorful Christmas-tree brooch or maybe some jingle-bell earrings. With Monica's short cropped hair and sharp angular face, jingle-bell earrings would have made her look cute. Human. Like she might actually be approachable or something.

"I heard she fired someone for being three minutes late to a meeting," Jeannie added.

Troy winced. "I don't think that's true."

"Well, I don't intend to find out firsthand. I avoid that

woman like bleach on jeans. I'll catch up with Santa later."

Jeannie turned her attention back to all that was fun and exciting about the evening, opting not to worry about Ice Queens and Santa Clauses for now. In a way, tonight was *her* night, her chance to shine after spending three years working hard to keep the company's engine running while her coworkers took the spotlight. At a seemingly endless stream of company functions and quarterly meetings, she'd smiled, cheered and clapped as the agents celebrated sales, as accountants were applauded for successful audits and year-end closes, as IT lauded new system releases. As an admin in Operations, her work was never celebrated even though it was the clerical staff like her that helped the others be so successful.

Jeannie's father would probably tell her a job is a place to earn money, not praise, but just once, she wanted to know what it was like to be on the receiving end of that simple recognition. That wasn't selfish, was it?

"Speaking of catching up later, I, um, was wondering if one of these days you'd like to—" Troy began, but she didn't hear the rest. At that moment, Gordy stopped the music and announced that their CEO, Mr. Stryker, was taking the stage to make a speech.

Jeannie smoothed her hair and checked her clothing, wanting to make sure she didn't have brownie crumbs on her reindeer sweater when Mr. Stryker turned all eyes to her in thanks for arranging the party.

"Are Rudolph's noses blinking?" she whispered to Troy, turning her face close to his so he could get a good look at her earrings.

He blushed and stuttered before finally understanding what she was talking about. "The earrings," he said. "Yeah, they're blinking."

"Thanks," she whispered then turned her attention back to Stryker and his speech.

"Did everyone survive the snowstorm?" Mr. Stryker asked the crowd. "I don't know about you, but every day that I have to shovel snow makes me wish I had a shorter driveway."

Laughter swept through the room and someone behind her muttered, "Like Stryker actually shovels his own snow."

A couple people chuckled to themselves but Jeannie ignored it and listened intently.

"Although, some of us are smarter than others," Stryker went on. "Monica got stuck in Florida, the poor thing, having to deal with all that sunshine while we were snowshoeing our way through Chicago."

About half the crowd laughed while Monica stood there, a pasted smile chiseled on her face. It looked as though she'd lost the pricey Santa, but was quickly inheriting his rosy red cheeks.

"They'd closed O'Hare," she defended, apparently not understanding that he was only making a joke, but Jeannie didn't think Mr. Stryker heard her. Instead of responding he started in about a holiday trip from hell his family had taken back when his son, John Junior, was in grade school.

John, now grown and second in command at Stryker & Associates, stood near the stage, interjecting occasionally as his father told the story, and while they spoke, Jeannie smiled and waited patiently.

"Anyway," the man finally concluded, "I don't want to ruin a good party by talking too much. But we are only a couple weeks from year-end, and there are some people I want to recognize tonight."

Jeannie folded her hands in her lap and straightened in her seat.

"Where's Nick Castle?" Stryker said, and from a spot near the bar, Nick called back, "Right here, Chairman!"

Nick was one of the few sales agents daring enough to give Mr. Stryker a nickname. And from what Jeannie understood, he was one of the few who got away with it. Looking at the man, she suspected he got away with plenty. Nick had the charm, good looks and sharp wit to make a fast path directly to the head of the line. Some people even gossiped that he was better equipped than John Jr. to take over the company, but of course, Jeannie would never repeat it. John Jr. was sweet and kind. He always smiled and said hi when she passed him in the halls, and she liked that he was part of the company even though sometimes it didn't look as though he wanted to be.

"Does this make three years in a row or four?" Mr. Stryker asked, and Nick shrugged as though he had no idea what the man was referring to.

"It seems to keep happening, anyway," Mr. Stryker went on. "Nick Castle is ending another year as our top selling insurance agent."

People clapped and cheered as Nick took a bow, accepting the pats and handshakes he'd worked hard for—and Jeannie recalled a trip to Maui was also part of the prize. The sales force had always been the crown jewel of the company.

Stryker continued down the list of sales awards then moved on to announcements in the middle market, a few milestone anniversaries and some preliminary year-end results, before finally finishing with, "So that's it. There's good food, music, plenty of drinks. Let's get on with the celebration!"

Then she watched as he handed the microphone back to Gordy Goodnite and stepped down from the stage.

As the voice of Bing Crosby filled the room with Christmas cheer, the words repeated in her thoughts.

A job is where you go to make money, not praise.

It did little to ease the lump in her throat or the weight of disappointment from her shoulders, and as she sat there still holding her hands in her lap, she fought the urge to run out of the room in tears.

It doesn't matter, she told herself. After all, it wasn't like people didn't know who organized the party. She'd sent out questionnaires and was the recipient of the RSVP list. Everyone in this room knew she was the one to make all this happen, so she really hadn't needed Stryker to restate the obvious.

She took a breath and the lump eased a little.

Of course, everyone appreciated her efforts, she reassured herself. The night was young, and she'd spent most of it either handling the last-minute details or sitting on the sidelines watching it go by. If she just got up and mingled a bit, she'd get plenty of the thanks she'd hoped for.

"So, anyway," Troy began, "as I was saying. I was wondering if—" He cleared his throat.

"Jeannie, the bartender's asking for you." Jeannie looked up to see one of the accounting managers standing over her. "He's got questions as to how much to serve, things like that. You might want to get over there."

"Sure." She glanced at Troy as she rose from her seat. "Sorry, what were you saying?"

Troy shook it off. "I'll catch up with you later." He smiled. "Go do your stuff, Chairman."

She studied his face for a moment—he was handsome, in a shy, clumsy kind of way. Troy was a nice man and she appreciated his cute words of support.

"Thanks, Troy," she said, forcing a smile on her face to drown out the remnants of disappointment. And then she went off to do what she did best.

Here Comes Santa Claus

1

"OUR FAMILY PHOTO IS scheduled for Thursday afternoon, so I'll need you at the house by twelve at the latest."

Monica Newell sat at her big mahogany desk in her office on the thirty-seventh floor of Chicago's Willis Tower listening to her mother go over the holiday plans.

"Remember, we're all wearing green this year," her mother went on. "You got the color swatch I sent, right?"

"Yes, it came in the mail last week."

"Make sure you find the right shade." Her mother added hopefully, "Or you could let me pick out a sweater for you. Really, that would be so much easier."

"I can pick out my own sweater," Monica affirmed, though it was likely pointless. She suspected her mother had already bought the perfect green sweater for the family photo and had it on hand in case whatever Monica showed up with was deemed unsuitable. Perfection was Phyllis Newell's way. Monica may have earned the position of chief financial officer for one of Chicago's oldest insurance agencies, but that title held no rank when pitted against the Newell family matriarch.

"If you must," Phyllis said through a sigh. "Just make

sure you don't buy a V-neck. You know how unflattering they look on you."

Monica smiled tightly. "Of course."

She made notes as her mother continued to jot off the holiday schedule—five days of meticulously arranged events that would keep the entire family busy through the holidays. The way Phyllis treated the Christmas season one would think the earth would implode if a single toast was so much as missed. Everything *had* to go a certain way and everyone *had* to be there. If not—well, up to this point, no one had dared to find out what would happen.

"On Friday we have to move up Christmas Eve brunch an hour because your father has a call to China he apparently can't get out of," Phyllis went on, the disappointment clear in her tone. "And did I tell you that Michael didn't get that big account he's been working on?"

"No, I hadn't heard."

Monica's brother owned a commercial real estate firm in Manhattan and had been spending the past six months trying to nail down a sales contract with a large downtown developer.

"Be a dear and don't mention it," Phyllis said. "It's a sensitive subject and the holidays are a time for cheer."

"I won't."

As her mother went on Monica eyed the crystal clock on her desk. The company Christmas party had started almost an hour ago. By now, even John Stryker would be there taking inventory of the staff. She didn't want to be the only executive missing from the room. John felt company functions played an important role in fostering teamwork at Stryker & Associates. Employees bowing out—particularly anyone on his senior leadership team—were highly frowned upon.

"So you'll be flying into LaGuardia when?" Phyllis asked.

"I'm hoping for Wednesday night, but it might be Thursday morning."

"You should come in Wednesday. I'd hate to have you looking harried for the photo after trying to rush here Thursday morning, and you never know what traffic could be like on 95."

"I'll do my best."

She listened patiently as her mother went over the last few details then promised to call back next week to further finalize the plans, and after the two women shared good-byes, Monica was done for the day, finally able to head upstairs to the company's holiday party.

Quickly, she touched up her makeup and made her way to the makeshift ballroom, pleased to see the party was just starting. People were still getting their food and eating, which meant she hadn't missed anything important. Breathing a sigh of relief, she stepped into the room, tossing off a few casual greetings to her associates and making her presence known.

Her assistant, Laura, slid up beside her. "You made it. I was about to come up and see if you needed a hand."

"I had to tie up some loose ends, but I think I'm done for the day."

"Good. Come eat."

Laura led her to the buffet table, where the two women picked up plates and surveyed the selections.

Laura pointed to various items. "Get some of Leonora's lumpia before it goes. They're delicious. The meatballs are sweet and sour, and that custard-looking thing is an egg dish Carol Peterson brought in."

Monica crinkled her nose. "What's in it?"

"Vegetables and some kind of meat. Pork, maybe. I'm not sure, but people have said it's good."

Monica picked up a lumpia but decided to pass on the custard. Instead, she searched the table for something more recognizable when her eyes zeroed in on a familiar white box with a signature LB logo on top.

She gasped. "Are those petits fours from Lady Baltimore?"

She opened the lid and the little chocolate delights winked back.

"Nick Castle brought those."

Nick, you prince.

She set one on her plate, bit her lip and dared to take one more. In her world, chocolate was a precious gem and Lady Baltimore petits fours were the Hope Diamond. Her opinion of the buffet table was definitely perking up.

She picked through the rest of the buffet then spent the next half hour mingling with the staff and chatting with her managers. By the time Monica finished eating and swallowing down a glass of white wine, she found herself alone by the windows reflecting on this past week of deadlines and snowstorms and the rush to scramble together preliminary year-end reports she'd be spending her weekend reviewing. It had been a stressful week. *But it had sure started out well, hadn't it?*

A faint smile curved her lips as she recalled her trip to Florida and the Chicago snowstorm that had left her stranded at JAX and spending the night in an airport hotel.

In the arms of the sexy cowboy she'd met only hours before.

She tingled just thinking about him, not only from the memory of how he'd masterfully pleasured her body, but also by the sheer lasciviousness of having a one-night stand with a virtual stranger. Her mother would faint at the notion, not to mention the bulk of her staff, most of whom looked up to her as the model of ultraprofessionalism.

Up until Monday night, Monica hadn't been the type to engage in such a sexual tryst—with a common Texas ranch hand, no less! She'd fit sex and relationships very neatly into her life much like she organized her closets and set aside time for yoga. Men had always been carefully selected from an assortment of business associates and partners in the industry. And while each and every one of them had been logical and well-suited, none had stirred the coals like the Stetson-wearing stranger she'd met in the airport lounge.

It had been such a primal night of lust, unearthing passion so hot it had literally scared her into fleeing in the wee hours of the morning, leaving only a terse note of thanks for the good time.

It was shameless, really. She would never treat an acquaintance so dismissively, much less a man she'd made love to, but she'd panicked. She'd never had stranger sex before, had no idea how to handle the morning after, so instead of tackling the situation with the same confident professionalism she held in the boardroom, she'd ducked out like a frightened teen, too awkward and embarrassed to do anything more.

But if she had, if maybe she'd walked away with a phone number or a way to get back in touch, she might have reserved the chance to meet up with her mystery cowboy again. Instead, her secret lover would have to remain a most delectable memory.

And, oh, what a memory.

"Are you enjoying the party?"

Monica pulled her thoughts to the present and looked up at the man in the red silk Santa suit.

"I am, thank you," she replied, raising a brow as she noted his appearance. He was an interesting rendition of Santa Claus, for sure, presumably hired by Jeannie as entertainment for the party.

The man moved his gaze over the room. "It's quite a festive night with all the lovely decorations, glorious food and sparkling music. Yet you look as though you're hundreds of miles away."

She crooked her mouth into a half smile. "Yes, I suppose for a moment I was."

He touched a hand to his full white beard. "Ah, to be many places at once. It's a common wish during the holidays." He handed her a candy cane, one of those cheap miniature ones sealed in a cellophane wrapper, and asked, "And if you could be anywhere this Christmas, where would you be?"

She considered all her choices—at home curled up on her couch with a cozy fire and a good book, back in Connecticut with her family, or maybe sharing a girls' weekend with her good friend Connie up in Ontario. But when she opened her mouth, the place most prominently on her mind tumbled from her lips.

"I'd love to be back in Florida."

He placed his palms to his fat belly and let out a roll of jolly laughter, just like every Santa in the movies. "Ah, yes, Florida. The state with plenty of warm days…*and even warmer nights, eh?*"

Her eyes widened. Had she heard him right? It was hard to tell over the music, but the knowing gleam in those bright blue eyes said she hadn't misunderstood.

"I'm afraid there's no room in my sleigh for travelers," he went on. "I can't take you to Florida, but I might be able to bring a little of Florida here to you."

He winked then glanced out the window, and she

followed his gaze, half expecting the dark night sky to open up to bright sunshine while rows of fluffy palm trees sprouted along Lake Michigan. He was a strange man and it was an even stranger comment, passing between them like a shared secret as if somehow this odd rental agency hire knew exactly what she'd been doing Monday night. But that was impossible. No one knew about the affair. She hadn't told her closest friend, much less anyone at the office.

She shook her head and brushed it off, feeling certain it was the culmination of a hectic week getting the best of her. Besides, she'd just been thinking about her Texan lover. It would be natural to put innuendo into anything the gentleman said. She assured herself it meant nothing, and that settled her nerves until she turned back to find him gone.

She darted her eyes around the room but he was nowhere. It was as if he'd disappeared. If it weren't for the candy cane still in her hand, she'd think the whole encounter had been a figment of her imagination, brought on by her tired state or maybe a bit of bad meat from that potluck buffet. But there it was in her hand, proof that the odd conversation truly happened.

Just then, the music stopped and John Stryker took the stage to begin his annual year-end speech, and as he spoke, her mind wandered to the jolly Santa's words.

Warm days and even warmer nights?

She might have passed it off as an innocuous comment if it hadn't been for the "nudge-nudge, wink-wink" look in his eyes. But how could anyone have possibly known what she'd done?

"I don't know about you, but every day that I have to shovel snow makes me wish I had a shorter driveway," John said from the stage, though she only half heard him, distracted by what was on her mind. It wasn't until he added, "Monica got stuck in Florida, the poor thing," that she glanced up startled and embarrassed as though, like the Santa, everyone in the room could read her thoughts and knew exactly what she'd done on her trip.

"They'd closed O'Hare," she stuttered, having no idea why she felt the need to defend herself. Nonetheless, the shrill in her voice drew half the room's attention to her, and now many were still staring at her, all wide-eyed and flustered, surely wondering if she'd lost her mind.

This was ridiculous. Her conversation with that silly Santa had set her off and now she was acting like a fool. As casually as possible, she ducked out of the party and down the hall to the bathroom, where she took a long breath and dabbed cold water on her face.

It was childish, carrying on like this over a one-night stand. So she'd had sex with a stranger. Women did it every day. And as a strong, successful executive in the business world, shouldn't she be able to enjoy a spicy night of pleasure without being overcome with guilt and fearing public scandal?

Okay, so maybe hot sweaty sex wasn't normally her style. Maybe her traditional prep-school upbringing had embedded in her a sense of propriety that didn't mesh well with steamy encounters with blue-collar working men. But hadn't she managed to deprogram most of those antiquated notions from her life?

Monday night, she certainly had. She'd found a man who was too sexy to deny, passionate and fiery, with a gritty smile and big brown eyes a girl could lose herself in. Kit Baldwin had been a riot in the lounge and a magician between the sheets, and she'd enjoyed every second of that flaming night in his arms.

It was only when he'd told her he'd wanted her number

before drifting off to sleep that she'd felt the clash of her prim and tidy world closing in on her. And in a sudden move of panic, she'd gathered her things and skipped out into the night.

Proof that she wasn't as pulled together as she'd like to believe.

And now she was standing here in the bathroom trying to fight off an overwhelming sense of indecency. What on earth was wrong with her?

Get a grip, Monica. It was just really good sex, for goodness' sake. And as for Kit, the man has surely forgotten all about you by now.

It was time she forgot about him.

She closed her eyes and restored her senses, taking calming breaths until she felt soothed and ready to go back to the party. It was that weird Santa Claus, she assured herself. There'd been something strange about the man and it had knocked her off her game—momentarily. But she was ready to take charge again. Feeling refreshed, she checked herself over in the mirror then headed back to the party.

She spent the next hour mingling with the employees, talking business and holiday plans. She congratulated Nick on winning this year's sales award and offered her thanks to those members of her staff who were working hard to meet the year-end deadlines. With the music and chatter and wine, she'd all but forgotten about Florida and her steamy night of passion. So she was completely unguarded by the time she heard John's voice over her shoulder.

"Monica, if you've got a second, I have someone I'd like you to meet."

Without hesitation, she turned and smiled, only to find herself staring into a set of familiar big brown eyes.

"Monica Newell, this is one of my favorite clients, Kit Baldwin." John gestured to Kit. "Kit, meet our chief financial officer, Monica Newell."

2

Kit grinned as he shook Monica's hand, disappointed to see shock in those beautiful green eyes instead of the delighted surprise he'd hoped for, but he wasn't deterred. Good fortune was following him tonight, and he was pretty sure that by the end of the evening, he'd turn that panicked expression into the sultry look he preferred.

"Ms. Newell, it's a pleasure," he offered brightly.

"Mr. Baldwin," she replied, nervously darting her eyes between the two men.

"Kit's been a long-time client of ours," John said.

"A client," she chirped, her grip tightening at the word *client*. She held her mouth in a tight-lipped smile that didn't do much to hide the fright in her eyes, but only Kit seemed to notice. Without so much as a curious glance, John remained oblivious as he went on with the introductions.

"Kit owns Shelley Ranch."

Her eyelids fluttered. "I'm familiar with that account."

"It was named after my mother," Kit explained.

Some of the color was returning to her cheeks but it wasn't a friendly shade. Okay, so maybe he hadn't explained his connection to Stryker & Associates when he'd met her in the lounge Monday night. By the time they'd gotten to the subject of their careers, he'd already been half-crazy about her, bound and determined to spend some quality time with the sharp and sexy brunette. So when she'd mentioned the company she worked for and he'd clued in to the coincidence, he decided against revealing any pesky detail that might have stuck a pitchfork in his plans.

Judging by the look on her face, it probably hadn't been a good move.

"Kit called to say he was in town," John went on, "so I invited him to come join the party."

She pulled her hand away and fisted it at her side. "How lucky for us."

The corporate smile pasted on her face had grown so taut Kit feared her lips might split apart. She was holding up a decent front, but he knew as soon as he got her alone, he'd be facing some sharp words. And that was okay by him. He had a few questions of his own, starting with why she'd pulled a disappearing act on him Monday night.

It certainly wasn't because she'd been having a dull time. Kit didn't claim to be a psychic between the sheets, but he knew a satisfied woman when he saw her. Ms. Newell hadn't ducked out for lack of pleasure, so why she'd fled at all remained left to be explained.

As if luck kept answering his call tonight, a young man stepped up to John's side and muttered something about a call, prompting John to turn to Monica. "I need to handle this. Do you think you could show Kit to the bar and see that he gets a drink?" He gestured to the buffet. "There's food if you're hungry."

Kit grinned. "Don't worry about me. I'm easily entertained."

As soon as John stepped away Monica's chiseled smile vanished.

"A client?" she choked out under her breath. "You said you were a ranch hand."

"I said I worked on a ranch. You saw the scuffed boots and jeans and assumed that part yourself."

"You *own* the ranch."

He slipped her a friendly wink. "I hope that doesn't ruin the fantasy."

Her cheeks reddened and he almost thought she'd slap him, but he was saved by a couple who'd unwittingly moved within earshot, forcing her to step aside.

"You should have told me," she snapped after they'd taken a few steps away. "You knew I worked here yet you didn't say a thing."

"Would you have still spent the night with me?"

"Absolutely not!"

He shrugged. "Then I'm glad I kept my mouth shut."

Another group wandered into their space and in a huff, Monica gestured toward the bar. "I'll get you that drink, then you can tell me what you're doing here."

He followed her across the room, making use of the opportunity to appreciate that fine figure of hers. It was especially sweet from behind. The woman was tall and slim, a bit thinner than he preferred, but he suspected that came from too much work and too little fun—something he intended to rectify if he got what he came for tonight. Even so, she had it all right where he liked it. Put that together with razor-sharp smarts and fiery Irish blood and Monica Newell was exactly the type of woman he'd been waiting for.

He only needed to get *her* interested. Not a small task considering she was mad as hell, but Kit always had loved a challenge.

He ordered a scotch and she settled for wine, then they stepped to the windows, away from the crowd but not so far as to appear too intimate. Before she could scold him some more, he casually leaned close and asked, "What are you wearing under those sexy white slacks?"

Her eyes popped wide as saucers.

"Tell me it's not the white lacy thing you were wearing Monday night."

A wisp of recognition crossed her features, coloring those wide eyes and hinting at raw desire, but she quickly tamped it down. "What are you doing here?"

"Looking for a repeat performance."

"And you couldn't have simply called? You obviously knew how to find me."

"That wouldn't have been nearly as fun."

Those angry eyes narrowed. "Oh, so you enjoy watching me sweat."

He flashed his sexiest smile. "No, but I enjoy making you sweaty."

She opened her mouth then closed it, then opened it again but still didn't say a word. He couldn't be sure, but he thought he saw a distant glimmer of amusement strike the corner of her mouth but it was forced out by her stubborn determination.

"I want to see you again," he said, opting to get straight to the point of this visit.

He didn't know why Monica had taken off Monday night, but after the night they'd shared, he wasn't going to let her go without an argument. Even before they'd hit the hotel room, they'd been having a good time. In a matter of a couple short hours, he'd grown intrigued by her smarts and sharp wit, the quirky contrast between her ingrained manners and confident authority. She was a rare type who could strike a strong man down without a flinch yet still probably know the proper way to address the Queen of England. A cobra disguised as a doe, curious, complicated, and about the only woman he'd ever met who'd interested him enough to go running after.

And now that he'd found her, he wouldn't be quick to walk away.

"That's impossible," she said.

He took a sip of his drink and spoke over the glass. "On the contrary, I've got a hotel room downtown. Unless you'd be more comfortable at your place—though that would make it hard for you to pull another great escape again."

"There will be no repeat," she insisted under her breath.

"Why not? According to Stryker you're not married."

She gasped. "You asked Mr. Stryker if I was *married?*"

"I needed to know if I had a fighting chance. You still owe me an explanation for cutting out on me, by the way. I get that you're upset by me showing up like this tonight, but if you'd left me something more than 'thanks for the good time,' I might have just picked up the phone and called."

Finally, those flames in her eyes gave way to something a little more promising. It looked a lot like guilt, something he wasn't above exploiting if it got him the girl.

"You're right," she said. "I owe you an apology for that."

"I've got a number of ways you can repay me."

"Stop!" Her mouth quirked as though she were forcing back a grin, and it was then he knew he had her. He'd expected he might receive a brisk chill showing up the way he had tonight. He'd feared he would hit solid ice along with the harsh reality that the special spark that had ignited between them had been entirely one-sided. But despite her attempt at affront, it was obvious the woman was pleased to see him, leaving him relieved and more determined than ever to see where this might go.

He bent in and whispered close to her ear. "That's not what you were saying Monday night."

MONICA TRIED TO STAND firm, holding on to her anger for support, but darn if Kit wasn't getting to her using that sexy drawl and sparkling smile to chip away at her resolve. He'd slipped under her usual defenses with ease back at the airport, charming her out of her clothes before she could ask "your room or mine?" And now, with a hundred reasons to keep him at arm's length, she was once again biting back flutters and wondering if maybe she could indulge just one more time.

"I can't believe you discussed my personal life with my employer," she said, working hard to remind herself why this man was a walking hazard.

How could she ever maintain Mr. Stryker's respect if her love life became public knowledge—with a client, no less!

Stryker & Associates was a reputable and desirable firm to work for, but it was entirely old-school. Monica was the first woman to be appointed to the board of directors and still the only one holding a chair. She'd shattered a glass ceiling most considered impenetrable, and she'd done it by being better than the rest and remaining staunchly professional on the job. The female junior executives here looked up to her as inspiration for what they could achieve. She'd accomplished what others hadn't, but along with that accomplishment went a responsibility she couldn't take lightly.

And cavorting with a long-time client topped the list of dim-witted behavior.

"I only casually mentioned to John that I thought you were pretty and asked if you were spoken for," Kit explained. "How wonderful you feel naked is my business alone."

She felt an ulcer forming in her stomach. The man was so furiously composed, so absent of propriety, that it made her want to spit nails. Yet quite pathetically, it was that same dry sense of humor and boyish disregard for protocol that made him so ridiculously attractive.

As much as she hated to admit it, she'd liked that he was upbeat, reckless and fun—pretty much everything she wasn't. And just like she had Monday night in the lounge, she was having trouble keeping her distance. Even now, with her fingers itching to strangle him senseless, she was alternately pleased to see him. Like some helpless romantic, she was actually thrilled that he'd come chasing after her, even though she hadn't liked his methods.

"Relax," he assured her. "John has no idea we've even met. In fact, if you'd like I'll tell him I made a pass and you struck me down like lightning." He rubbed his chin. "Though that means we can't invite him to the wedding."

She let out an exasperated breath, not just from his inability to take this seriously but by the fact that his silly jokes actually charmed her. He was definitely not the type of man she ever thought she'd fall for—not that she was admitting such a notion now. Only that if she *was* to get serious about someone, she'd always assumed it would be with someone more…serious.

Despite it all, she couldn't stop her eyes from wandering along the lines of that strong stubbled jaw, over those talented lips, down that broad, muscled chest and beyond, gathering memories of their blissful night every step of the way. He'd been good. Really good. And now he was back, all sexy and confident and asking to do it again. How did she stand a chance against that?

"Dance with me," he muttered through a gaze just as steamy as her thoughts.

Only then did she hear the music from the stage—"Blue Christmas," a slow smoky version meant for snuggling close. She opened her mouth and tried to say no but her lips wouldn't form the words. Her body was too busy screaming yes. And in the wake of her indecision, he took her hand and led her to the dance floor.

He held her gently at her waist, heat resonating from his palms and tingling down to her toes. He kept at a respectable distance, giving the appearance of a polite dance among associates to the common bystander. But there was nothing polite about the hunger in his gaze or the way it made her feel. That was Grade A carnal and primal, and as they rocked to the music, a giddy dizziness came over her.

"Spend the night with me," he uttered quietly. "Come with me tonight and let me wake up with you in the morning."

Immediately, desire waged war with her senses. This was wrong in so many ways. The man was a client, and though there was no corporate policy against dating clients, it broke every personal rule she had.

"I've got a number of things we didn't get to Monday night." Then he bent close and whispered a sampling, spreading heat through her veins.

Stop it, Monica, she insisted through the fog. *You've got a thousand reasons why going home with Kit Baldwin would be a horrible idea.* Though off the top of her head, she couldn't recall a single one. His woodsy aftershave kept flooding her senses with the memory of his body in hers, how deliciously wonderful he'd felt and how much she'd ached to have him again. She'd been so easily seduced by his rugged good looks and fun, casual style. It was as if he'd found a switch he could turn on with a flick of his finger. She'd thought she was a stronger woman, presumed she'd end up the one in control of her relationships, yet here she was a second time, entranced by his simple touch and helpless against his wicked offerings.

From the corner of her eye she spotted John Stryker stepping back into the room, and his attention on her and Kit should have been a sign that she needed to gather her senses and walk away. But with Kit's gorgeous brown eyes pointed in her direction—and promising undiluted pleasure—her good intentions crumbled under the weight of lust and greed.

"Okay," she heard herself utter. "Let's get out of here."

3

"WHERE'S YOUR BEDROOM?"

Kit stepped through the entry and into the living room of Monica's high-rise apartment and scanned the layout as he went. The furnishings were exactly as he'd expected—sleek, orderly, with touches of Asia and Europe that looked authentic but not decorative. Oversize windows offered a view of the Chicago skyline that would be nice to relax to someday, but right now he had a more urgent need—namely getting naked with a stunning brunette as quickly as possible.

"You wouldn't care for a drink first? 'My, what a fine night this is? Nice place you've got here?'" Monica teased.

He slipped a hand around her waist and pulled her close. "You underestimate how badly I want you." Then he showed her by cupping her cheek and closing his mouth over hers.

With that one connection his spirit righted, placed back on its axis after being knocked off-kilter Monday night. Something had clicked that night, a feeling that he'd found something special, and despite his efforts to put their encounter in the past, he'd realized pretty quickly that it wasn't going to happen.

He liked Monica Newell. He didn't know how it could feel so solid in a single night together, but he'd known she was the one he wanted. And when Kit felt something this sure, he wasn't going to let it go.

He slid his hands up under her sweater and found skin, then groaned at the pure luxury of the silky feel beneath his fingers. He loved the fact that her long legs squared her body with his—thighs against thighs, breasts against chest, heat against heat—and he loved her tender response when all those parts came together. He clasped her waist and made her shiver, touched her breasts and made her moan, hungry need boiling through him with every simple press. He hardened instantly, slipped his palms down around her ass and pulled her close against his erection, and she sighed.

"How do you get me so hot so fast?" she whispered against his lips.

For the first time in his life, he had no witty comeback. Truth was he'd wondered the same thing and had come up with nothing other than this must be what genuine need felt like.

With quick fingers, he unclasped her slacks, letting them drop from her waist where they pooled around her feet. And when he tucked a hand into her panties he nearly lost himself from the wet readiness that greeted him.

He muttered off a curse, slipped a finger where his cock ached to follow, and the breathy gasp that escaped her throat propelled him into action. He ground against her, smoothing his fingers over the soft spot between her legs, not intending to move so quickly but unable to stop the momentum. He dropped to his knees, pulling her red laced panties down with him, and when her musky scent of sex filled his nostrils he couldn't help but dip in for a taste.

He nibbled at her mound, taking light bites and pressing kisses to the inner flesh of her thighs, trying to tease her slowly and draw out the pleasure, but the burn for more kept pushing him to drive harder. Helpless against it, he slipped his tongue between her folds, feeling a surge of pleasure when her clit pulsed against his tongue and she groaned in ecstasy.

Her long, slim fingers tangled in his hair, nudging him against her and coaxing him to keep going, as if he'd needed the prod. He'd started something he couldn't stop, and with desire doing the driving, he dove in and stroked her sex.

Greedily, he kissed and sucked and licked, her fists clasping him hard as her legs began to tremble. Her sweet taste fueled him, urging him on with the scent of impending climax that absorbed through his lungs and pooled heavy in his loin. Her breath came out in pants, growing shallow and dire with every lap of his tongue. And when her tender flesh swelled against his lips, he grabbed her hips and held tight.

Her release was swift and hard, quaking through her body and shooting pulse after pulse of sensation straight to his cock. He'd always enjoyed pleasuring a woman, but this one seemed to give him an extra dose of satisfaction. There was something empowering in taking that staunchly held control and crumbling it down to raw lust. And when he did, the woman he found underneath excited and seduced him.

She slid to her knees and settled against him, neither of them having the strength to move to the bedroom. Instead, he pulled her red sweater over her head and tossed it aside, then guided her down to the carpet right where they'd stood.

His heart beat like thunder, need straining against his jeans as he yanked a condom from his pocket and quickly went to work shucking his clothes. With the flush of orgasm still coloring her cheeks, those green eyes remained hungry, prompting him to keep going as she unclasped her bra and bared herself to him.

He bent in and took her modest breast in his mouth, unable to deny himself for the briefest of moments as he released the last button of his shirt and tossed it aside. Sex was supposed to satisfy a soul, but when it came to Monica, all it seemed to do was leave him greedy. The more he took the more he ached, one climax only fueling the need for another. So with the last of the barriers tossed aside, he quickly sheathed himself and rose over her.

She eyed his stiff shaft and uttered, "Yes," spreading her thighs and arching her back to receive him. And through the rawness in her voice, he saw the inner soul of this sharply mannered executive, the bare woman underneath the corporate facade. She was sexy as hell, and he relished his power to uncover her, to draw out that piece that she kept so tidily wrapped up to everyone else.

He slipped between her legs and pushed inside, nearly bursting as he watched that sensual woman unravel. Those lustrous lips parted as the length of him filled her, thrusting deep until his cock was fully seated. And when he began to rock and stroke, a warm calm smoothed her sharp features.

He pressed his lips to hers and let their bodies tangle together, grinding toward a climax that would take them both over the edge. He rolled her over on top of him, taking her breasts in his hands as she rode him, that lustrous heat encasing him and pushing him to the brink as those emerald eyes soaked up his gaze. This was a connection more than sex, he knew. He'd felt it that first night and sensed it again, something strong crossing between them. And when release found them and their bodies crashed together, he knew she felt it, too. It was desire beyond attraction, want that bordered on obsession. And something he had no intention of walking away from.

He rolled back over and drove the last of the climax until his body was sated, heart thudding wildly against her breast and his lips gently stroking the sensitive space under her ear. They stayed that way for what seemed like hours, neither speaking, only breathing and basking in the pleasure of their union. And only when he feared his weight crushing her did he roll to his side and draw her close, cradling her head on his shoulder and closing her into his arms.

"I still don't know where your bedroom is," he muttered.

Her smoky laugh brushed warmly across his chest. "You did fine without it."

"That was just a warm-up." He tugged her chin up to his and kissed her on the lips. "For everything else I've got planned, I think we'll want to get more comfortable."

"WHAT DO YOU DO FOR fun, Monica?" Kit asked as the two lay in her bed sharing a glass of cognac.

"You mean, besides picking up strange men in airport lounges?"

He winced. "I'd like to think that's not a common pastime."

She reached over him and set the glass on the nightstand then sidled up close, resting her head on his broad shoulder and circling her leg around his. It was nearing 10:00 p.m. and they were entering their third hour of naked bliss. Monica would have called it record-breaking sex if Kit hadn't already treated her to a marathon evening four nights earlier. Up against that, tonight was simply par for a very delicious course—one she wouldn't mind playing again and again if she could only get beyond the business relationship that still wasn't settling well with her.

But that was a quandary better left for another hour. Right now, she intended to enjoy as much of the generous lover as possible before morning brought up reality with the sun.

"The other night you said you loved traveling," he went on. "I noticed some pieces in your living room looked Japanese and Scandinavian."

His eye for art impressed her. "Yes, once a year I take a trip abroad. I spend most of the rest of my time planning it. It's a passion of mine, researching cities, finding the exact perfect accommodations, planning meals and putting together a schedule."

She rested casually against him and told him about the countries she'd visited, sharing stories about some of the sights she'd seen and places she hoped to go in the future.

"One place I need to return to is Italy," she said. "I'd completely misjudged the amount of time I'd need to see the sites on my itinerary. In the end it wasn't enough, but now that I know, I can do a better job planning out the next trip."

"Have you ever just packed a bag and taken off?"

"What do you mean?"

He shrugged. "No schedule. No plans. Just go where the day takes you."

She tried to imagine that but couldn't. Granted, she knew people who traveled on the fly like that, but Monica preferred knowing exactly where she was going and what she would be doing.

"I like to be a little more organized than that."

"It's not about organization, it's about adventure. One night you might find yourself in a hostel. The next you could be the personal guest of a family you just met." He sipped from the glass of cognac then set it back on the table. "Some people find it exciting."

Monica shook her head. "I'd find it unsettling."

He slid lower under the blankets, turning to face her and drawing her close so that their noses nearly touched. "You should give it a try. Come out to my ranch in Austin."

"Oh, I don't know."

"I can have my pilot ready to fly out in an hour."

"Your pilot. You have a plane?"

"With my lifestyle, it's a necessity." He kissed her nose and brushed a tender finger across her cheek. "I promise to have you back at work bright and early Monday morning."

She blanched. "I couldn't possibly."

"Why not?"

"A thousand reasons. I've got a preliminary report to read for one. It requires my comments and narrative."

"Read it on the plane. It will work out good. I've got calls to make anyway."

She pulled away and sat up. "It could take hours. I'd already cleared my weekend to get through it."

"I've got a nice quiet study at the ranch."

"But that would be rude. I can't come as a guest to your home then spend half the weekend ignoring you."

"I'd like to think of you as more than just my guest. And as far as ignoring me, as long as you have dinner with me and sleep in my bed I'll be satisfied."

She clasped the blankets to her chest, feeling panicked

and silly and nowhere near ready to entertain the idea of a trip. She hadn't even come to terms with tonight's encounter, what it meant about their relationship—if it *was* a relationship. And if it was, she still wasn't sure it should be. For the moment, she'd accepted a one-night stand, though technically now it was two. Jetting off to Texas for the weekend?

He tugged the blanket off her shoulder and began pressing kisses up her forearm toward her neck, circling that tongue ever so lightly, which only scattered her thoughts more.

"I'd have to pack," she started. "I'd have to consider what to bring. I need my laptop. I left it at the office. That alone will take, ooohhhh—" He'd found a sensitive spot right at the tip of her spine.

"You know what I think?" he asked.

She lolled her head to the side while he spoke between kisses.

"I think your problem isn't your laptop or packing or being a rude guest. I think you don't like surprises." He pressed his lips to each vertebrae, slowly trailing his way down her spine. "You need to always stay in control and you can't do anything that isn't precisely planned and thoroughly considered."

She scoffed. "That's my mother, not me."

He slipped a warm hand over her breast as those succulent lips neared her tailbone. "So that's where you get it from."

"I'm nothing like her. She's a homebody, I'm an executive." His mouth touched the curve of her butt before he turned and went back the way he came. "Honestly, the woman drives me crazy. She'd had my life planned out while I was still in the womb. To this day it burns her that

I didn't settle in the Hamptons with a surgeon husband and two-point-seven kids."

"I'm sure your mother's proud of you," he uttered.

"Maybe, but she wasn't pleasant to live with. I don't know how my father handles it. Everything has to be done exactly her way. She has ideas in her head how everything should be, and heaven help the person who tries to change her mind once it's made up. You should have seen her planning a family reunion last year. Every minute of the day was—"

She stopped and gasped. "Oh, my, I really *am* like her."

"I'm sensing similarities," Kit said casually.

Monica stared blankly at the shelves on the wall—the ones she'd meticulously placed and decorated with books stacked exactly so. She recalled the day the maid dusted and mistakenly put things back in the wrong place. She'd noticed immediately, couldn't do another thing until she'd taken it all down and put it back the way she had it.

How could she have gotten to this age and never seen it?

Everyone always said she was exactly like her father. And in many ways she was. But in the face of this discussion she realized that she'd also picked up a few traits from her mother, too—and not the ones she'd preferred. The perfectionist, unbending and controlling—Monica wouldn't have believed it, yet here she was, shooting down Kit's suggestion exactly the same way and using the same unyielding attitude she would have expected of her mother. She didn't want to be that person.

"I can't believe this," she uttered. "I sound exactly like her."

Kit took her hand and pressed kisses to her fingers. "Then I like her already."

Monica shook her head. "No, not in a good way."

She'd never noticed the similarity before, but it seemed obvious now, and her reaction was nothing short of pure horror.

"Let's do it," she said. "Let's go to Austin."

She tossed the blankets, intent to prove that she didn't have to be that person. The best part of self-awareness was the ability to make a change, right? So just because she'd inherited a few of her mother's least desirable traits didn't mean she had to accept them. But when she scooted from the bed Kit clasped her forearm and pulled her back.

"What are you doing?" she asked. "I thought you wanted to take me to your ranch."

"In a minute."

He nudged her down and began ravaging her like he'd done several times this evening. "First, I need to make love to you again."

Heat spilled through her as flesh connected with flesh and those dark eyes took on the familiar glaze of sultry intent.

"What's this? Another sudden change in plans?" she asked.

He dipped his mouth to hers and spoke through a kiss. "Yes. You're incredibly sexy when you act on impulse."

4

MONICA WOKE UP TO THE smell of coffee, bacon and something deliciously sweet. Pancakes? Blinking her eyes open, she looked around the large room for a clock and found none. Her only clue as to the time was the sunlight peeking through the wood shutters, which didn't tell her much.

She reminded herself that it didn't matter. She was on a new quest to be less rigid, and things like hours and minutes on her days off weren't supposed to matter. Pulling herself from the bed, she padded across Kit's bedroom and found the overnight bag she'd thrown together. Then she washed up and dressed before venturing out to track down the source of those delectable smells. On the way she gathered her watch and was startled to see it was after nine, but considering how late they'd gotten to bed, she supposed it was reasonable. It was nearly two when they'd finally turned in, later than that when they'd actually gotten to sleep.

A smile curved her lips. A late night indeed, but well worth it.

She stepped out into the large great room. It was bigger than it seemed the night before. The decor was rustic and manly, comfortable and casual. A true reflection of Kit, as she was learning, and it recalled the old saying that everything was bigger in Texas. His house and his ranch—and a few other things—most definitely were.

"I knew the bacon would draw you out," Kit said from the stove as she stepped up to the stone counter and took a seat at the bar. "Or was it the coffee?"

He stood barefoot at the stove wearing only a pair of worn jeans and a button-down flannel shirt that looked soft to the touch. His dark hair was still damp from a shower and through the heavenly scent of bacon and maple, the fresh odor of soap and aftershave seeped through. He'd left his shirttails out, giving him that rumpled look she found delectably attractive. Why she'd always gone for the polished look she'd never know. This easy, rugged strength was so much sexier.

"It was the smell of maple syrup," she said. She eyed the feast he was constructing and her stomach growled. "Tell me you've got fluffy carbs for me to pour it on."

"Pancakes are in the warmer."

She brightened. "If they're good, I'll ask you to marry me."

He smiled and winked. "I'll say yes."

She laughed at the joke, even though the look in his eyes said he might be serious. Instead, she focused on the coffee he placed in front of her.

"I've set you up in my office," he said, placing platters in front of them before joining her at the bar for breakfast. Grinning, he added, "I suppose you didn't get as much work done on the plane as you'd hoped."

No, she hadn't. Once they'd settled on his private jet she'd opened her laptop and tried to read through the reports, but she'd underestimated how sexy Kit would be on his phone talking business in that smoky Texas drawl. She'd kept forcing her attention back to her numbers and he'd kept yanking it away, and with one thing leading to another, she ultimately ended up a card-carrying member of the mile-high club.

"I had some trouble concentrating," she replied, returning his knowing look.

"Well, that won't be a problem today. The study is quiet and I won't even be within earshot."

"What are your plans?"

He talked around a mouthful of scrambled eggs. "I'm working on a project out in the barn. When you want a break, come out and I'll show it to you."

She took a bite of pancake—fluffy enough to marry him, it turned out—and replied, "Fair enough."

UNFORTUNATELY, TWO HOURS later she was no less distracted than she'd been on the plane. She'd gotten through the reports, made some cursory notes, but every time she started her write-up her mind wandered to the glorious time she was having with Kit and how much she really liked him.

They had more in common than she'd assumed that first night. At the time, she'd thought she was only dealing with attraction and sexual desire, but the more she got to know him, the more she began to recognize genuine affection. It was an experience that both excited her and left her a little afraid. Up to now, her life had been simple. She had her job and her travels, neither one interfering with the other. Now a man had come into that world, one who didn't even live in Chicago, and her boat was starting to rock.

She wondered what he was doing. What was his project in the barn?

Then she scolded herself and put her focus back on work. John was expecting her briefing Monday morning, and she always provided him with the materials beforehand so he could review them in advance.

But that was Monday, and technically she had plenty of time to put her presentation together. Even probably on the plane ride back to Chicago if she really focused and buckled down.

Biting her lip, she closed her laptop. She'd never made a habit of putting off work, not even back in college. She'd always preferred to get it done first and play later—if there was time left over. But it wasn't every day that a woman got whisked off in a private jet by a sexy cowboy to spend the weekend at his big sprawling ranch. It might never even happen again. So caution thrown aside, she left her write-up and set off to find him.

Despite several buildings on the property, she headed toward the one that most looked like a barn, pleased when she pulled open the door and found Kit inside. He was standing at a lathe, its motor whirring and sawdust flying as the machine spun what appeared to be a wooden table leg. He held a tool that was either smoothing or shaping the wood as it spun.

With her presence unknown, she stood and watched him work. The man was lethally handsome with his thick brown hair and solid square jaw. Though he shaved daily, his beard grew quickly, giving him a perpetually masculine look that she found deliciously attractive. He'd taken off the flannel shirt he'd worn at breakfast and was now clad in a T-shirt that showed off those muscled biceps she'd already grown so fond of. For several minutes she stood watching, listening to the country music from the radio, and as she took in the scene, she couldn't help but be amused over this odd situation she'd found herself in.

If someone had told her last week that she'd be standing in a barn outside Austin tapping her toes to honky-tonk music while her wealthy cowboy lover sanded table legs, she would have checked them for drugs. Yet here she was.

And she was enjoying it, too.

He shut off the machine and pulled off his safety glasses, and when he caught sight of her his face lit with a smile that touched her chest.

"Hey, sexy," he drawled.

KIT SLAPPED THE DUST from his hands and tugged Monica into a sensual kiss as soon as she came within reach. He knew he shouldn't be so insatiable. He didn't want her to think he only wanted her body, but he couldn't help it. He'd found an appetite for the beautiful brunette he couldn't seem to control.

Pressing his lips to hers, he found the sweet taste of maple sugar and it made him think of candy. He loved kissing her, loved having his hands on her and feeling those long fingers on him. It was a sugary treat he could get used to every day.

A low moan purred from her throat as she slid her hands up his chest, getting him hard and horny in one smooth stroke. And as he pulled her closer and dove in for something serious, he wondered where in his workshop might be the best spot for a quickie.

"You were going to show me your project," she uttered to his lips.

"Something better just walked in."

He slipped his hands up under her light cotton blouse and cupped her breasts in his palms, deciding that the workbench could be cleared pretty quickly. But then he remembered that Doug Rawlins, a mechanic, was due any minute to give him an estimate on one of his trucks.

Reluctantly, he pulled away. "You torment me, you know that?" he grumbled.

"I didn't ask you to stop."

"No, but I'm expecting company, and give me two more minutes near that sexy body of yours, we'll end up putting on quite a show."

"Hmm." She touched a finger to her lips. "I could do kinky, but I do draw the line at voyeurism."

His interest piqued. "How kinky?"

"Your project," she said, straightening her blouse and moving toward his lathe.

Storing that comment for later, he guided her toward another room, where he'd been finishing the desk he was working on. "It's a Christmas present for my niece."

Monica gaped as she stepped over and studied the piece. "You *made* this?"

Shrugging, he tried to brush off his boyish pride in impressing the woman. "I'm working on a matching chair, but I'm running out of time."

He stepped to the desk. It was pine with a beveled top and three drawers, simple in construction and stained in a light natural finish. What made it special was the carved roses around the drawer pulls, and seeing her reaction confirmed it had been worth the effort.

She ran a finger over the carvings. "You did this by hand?"

He nodded.

"Kit, it's beautiful. I'm sure she'll love it."

He scratched the back of his head. "Well, she might have to wait for it. Christmas is next weekend and I've got to be in Chicago and Omaha for half the week. I'm debating between canceling some important meetings or just giving her the desk and promising the chair after New Year's."

She balked. "You've got to do both."

Her insistence made him smile. He liked people who didn't accept limitations. It was one of the first things that had attracted him to her. Not many people could lift his own standards on what he was capable of, but he'd learned pretty quickly that Monica could be one of them.

"What's left to do?" she asked.

"Cassie, my niece, asked for pink flowers." He stepped to a table where he'd stored an array of craft paints and brushes. "The table needs one more undercoat then I need to figure how I want to paint the roses. I'll need a clear gloss over that, then I need to repeat the whole process for the chair."

"You know what would be pretty—" She stepped to the counter and surveyed his paints, and he watched as she grabbed a brush and a paper bag and began mixing colors.

Like a master, she created an almost identical replica of his roses on paper, using several shades of pink, white and red to add depth to the finished product. It blew away anything he'd been thinking.

"I had no idea you could paint."

"I minored in art in college. Economics, math and accounting could be grueling, and I needed an escape. And since I'm tone deaf, music was out." She nudged the paper toward him and spoke casually as though she hadn't just floored him with her artistry. "What do you think of something like this?"

"It would be beautiful."

"Then why don't you get back to work on your chair and let me finish the desk?"

He blinked. "You wouldn't mind? Sweetheart, I didn't bring you out here to help me finish my niece's Christmas present."

Stepping close, she pressed her palms to his chest and whispered. "It will cost you some serious sexual favors."

He circled his arms around her and wondered how many more wonderful surprises this intriguing woman had up her sleeve. He'd love to spend a lifetime finding out. But recognizing the need to take this slowly he kept those intentions to himself and instead kissed her gently on the cheek. "I'm going to have a hell of a time repaying you."

5

MONICA RELAXED ON THE floor of Kit's great room, enjoying the roaring fire in the fireplace while Kit rubbed her shoulders. It was early Sunday evening and they would be flying back to Chicago tonight, though if she could be granted one Christmas wish, it would be to stay here a few more days.

They'd spent yesterday and this morning finishing the desk for Kit's niece. Hardly a chore, she'd found the project relaxing and revitalizing. She hadn't dabbled with anything artistic since college. The moment she'd started her first internship at a New York investment firm, she'd been entirely focused on a career in finance. From that point on, her appreciation for art had been restricted to collecting pieces made by others, and she'd forgotten the joy of creating something herself.

In fact, she'd forgotten a lot of joys before spending these past few days with Kit. When they weren't busy in the barn, they were enjoying his delicious meals. They'd taken a long walk on his property down to the lake where he sometimes fished. They'd ridden one of his ATVs to the top of the ridge to view the sunset. And, of course, when they weren't doing those things, they were discovering the many ways they could pleasure each other in bed.

It was the type of weekend she could get used to, escaping the noise of the city for a simple weekend on a ranch, not to mention the wonderful company. And as Kit's fingers stroked pure luxury through her muscles, she wondered why this peach of a man hadn't already been snatched up by a deserving woman.

"Why aren't you taken?" she asked, lolling her head to the side as he dug those talented fingers into the curve of her neck.

"I've come close a couple times."

"You're a great catch. How could they let you get away?"

He laughed and kissed her bare shoulder. "Sweetheart, whether or not I'm a catch depends on what you're fishing for. I've got businesses in three states, a home in Texas and a sailboat down in Florida. I'm on the go a lot, and at first, women find that exciting. But eventually they want more than I can give."

He shifted behind her so that his legs straddled either side of her waist, and she leaned closer to him, using his thighs as armrests.

"Don't get me wrong," he went on. "I'm not a playboy. I'd love to find a life partner, someone to grow old with. But a woman who's looking for kids and peewee football and a man who's home every weekend ends up mighty frustrated. I can't do that kind of routine. I've got a brood of nieces and nephews from my two sisters, and I treat them as my own. But more than that, my lifestyle isn't suited to having children, and I don't really care to change it."

Monica understood completely. And she knew firsthand that most people didn't. She loved her family, adored spoiling her nieces and nephews, but she'd never wanted kids of her own. She knew what a sacrifice raising a child was, and hadn't wanted to give up so much of her independence. Some people called that selfish, but in her opinion, the selfless act was accepting her limitations and leaving the parenting to people who could truly devote themselves to the task.

"I'm afraid I broke a few hearts before realizing I was hooking up with the wrong type of women," he said.

"What type would you consider right?"

He leaned close and spoke low to her ear. "I've got a fetish for short-haired brunettes with pretty green eyes."

She smiled and sipped her wine.

"I do better with women who enjoy their independence," he went on. "I'd love to be a part of her life, don't mistake me. But I need to be an equal, not the focal point. I could just as well be the spouse at her corporate functions as her being the spouse at mine. I'm career-minded, one of my passions is my business, and while I like to take time off to relax, I can never fully step away from it. My ideal partner is one who understands that and can maybe even share in it."

She sighed and shook her head. "We really are perfect together," she muttered, not even realizing she'd said it out loud until Kit replied, "That's exactly what I think."

He circled his arms around her and she relaxed against his broad chest, allowing her head to rest on his shoulder as she contemplated this fast relationship growing between them. From the moment he first approached her in that airport lounge, she'd been smitten with the man, finding him both sexually alluring and devastatingly handsome. Now she was becoming more and more intrigued by what was inside. But what did that mean? Would it even be possible maintaining a long-distance affair? Would it be enough to have a man who popped in and out of her life when their schedules happened to mesh? Or could they manage more?

And then there was the pesky issue of his business relationship with Stryker. If she'd ever placed one thing high on her priority list, it was never to mix business with pleasure. This didn't just mix it, it emulsified it.

Unfortunately, she had more questions than answers. Ironic, considering that she'd hoped spending the weekend with Kit would help get him out of her system. Instead, he'd only managed to sink in further.

"Come spend Christmas with me," he said.

She laughed dismissively. "That's impossible."

"Why? You did such a beautiful job on my niece's present I'd love for you to be there when she sees it. Besides," he said, kissing the base of her neck, "I can't think of a better present than you in my bed."

She shook her head and sat upright, turning to face him. "I couldn't possibly spend the holidays with you. I'm due in Connecticut Wednesday night. My mother has plans that can't be changed."

He shrugged as though this were a simple discussion about where to meet for lunch. "So spend the days up until Christmas Eve with your family and I'll fly you down to Austin in time for Christmas dinner."

She backed up, feeling the need to make some space as the moment of truth she'd been avoiding swept up to greet her. "It's out of the question," she said, recognizing by the look in his eyes that this was a conversation about more than just the upcoming holiday.

He wanted to talk about tomorrow, and the next day, and the next, to establish where this relationship was going and how they could make it work. But she didn't have answers to any of that. She was only just absorbing the idea of a real relationship here. She wasn't at all ready to start making plans—especially ones that interfered with her holiday traditions.

Tomorrow morning she'd be back at work in her old environment and her familiar life. It would be her opportunity to think clearly and get a better perspective on all this. Until that happened she couldn't begin to entertain thoughts of anything beyond this weekend.

"My mother would have a heart attack if I cut my visit short, especially at this late date."

"That control thing. I remember." The man lay sprawled across the rug, propped up on one elbow and sipping his bottled water as if this whole conversation was no big deal. And she supposed that for him it wasn't. He owned his own business that allowed him to do whatever he pleased. He wasn't a woman trying to make a name for herself in an old-school corporate world. She doubted he could even fathom a life that required putting up appearances and maintaining a level of professionalism over and above her male counterparts.

"It's not just that," she said. "You're a client of my company. As much as I enjoy what we've found here, I'm still not comfortable with that relationship."

"That's an easy one to resolve. If I have to choose between you and Stryker I'll move my business to another firm tomorrow."

"You can't!" Her heart began to pound. This was exactly the type of thing she feared and precisely why she avoided entanglements like this. Losing Kit's account because of her would be unconscionable. She'd be humiliated in the face of John and the other board members.

She set down her wine. "If you pull your account it will be my fault. How could you do that to me?"

He smiled and tugged her back toward him, closing the space between them and running a calming finger across her chin. "I'll never do anything to jeopardize your career or your image with the company. I'm only saying that you're more important to me than my business dealings with Stryker. If the connection makes you uncomfortable, we'll figure a way to get around it."

He kissed her, leveling his gaze with hers to express the sincerity in his words, and though it eased her slightly, she still couldn't get past the fear that they were playing with fire. Up to now, her career had always been her top priority, her comfort zone even. She didn't dabble with anything that might interfere with it. But now she was feeling the real pull to try to blend a relationship into the mix. It made her feel unsteady, uncertain even. Kit's connection with her company only complicated things. This wasn't something she could absorb in a two-day weekend.

"It's too much, too fast," she admitted.

His response was that casual calm that both infuriated and reassured her. "Then we'll slow down."

Easy, just like that. But why did she feel as though none of it would work out quite so simply?

"If you need more time, we'll take more time. I'm not going anywhere." He tugged her down on the rug then kissed her gently, soothing her fraying nerves under the warmth of the crackling fire. "I'll be in Chicago until Tuesday morning. Will you have dinner with me tomorrow night?"

"Tomorrow night?"

She tried to think about her schedule, but that got difficult when he nudged her tank top up and began circling his tongue around her navel. This was exactly what got her into this predicament in the first place. Every time Kit wanted something from her, all he had to do was scramble her thoughts with those talented lips and she lost her ability to think straight.

"Tomorrow night," he said, dipping his hand down under her sweats and cupping the heat between her thighs.

He slipped a finger between her folds and all the worry on her brow drained away to pure pleasure. It wasn't fair, his ability to win a discussion through this sinful distraction, but heck if she could work up the argument to stop him. He was too good and her body was too willing.

Propped on his elbow, he wrapped his lips around her breast and sucked while his finger began circling her most sensitive spot. "Ohhhh, tomorrow," she groaned, parting her legs and offering him access.

He replied with a gentle bite to her nipple.

Threading her fingers through his hair, she closed her eyes and listened to his sensual moans as he worked her body to another peak. They shed their clothes, pulled pillows from the couch to craft a bed on the floor in front of the big stone fireplace. Then he filled her, using his hard length and soft touches to take them both to the edge and over.

And with her thoughts now vacant of anything other than the luxury of his naked body over hers, he bent close to her ear and said, "I'll take that as a yes."

6

MONICA STEPPED DOWN the hall to John's office Monday morning feeling woefully ill-prepared. She never did send him a preliminary report. During her weekend with Kit, she'd shamelessly brushed off the task, continually telling herself she still had time—up to the point that she'd woken up this morning to realize time had run out. Now she had to face walking into John's office with only some cursory notes on a report she should have had memorized inside out.

She hated the vulnerability of not being on top of her game. To her it was like walking into a room naked or stepping out onto the windy ledge of a high-rise building. Yet even with her current state of unease, she knew she'd do it all again if given the chance.

Despite her suffering now, her weekend with Kit was the most fun she'd had since her trip to Morocco last summer, and it had made her realize that she needed more from life than her job and an annual vacation. In between trips abroad, she wanted those sensual nights with a sexy man who made her laugh. She wanted to explore the side of herself that wasn't the corporate executive—the woman with a creative flair and a love of nature, the stargazer who loved old movies and might actually consider buying a pair of purple cowboy boots. The woman with talents and secrets and friends to share them with.

She didn't see that woman often enough, only a few times a year when she got away from it all. And after spending the weekend with Kit, she realized those rare ventures into the open weren't nearly enough. She wanted more, and she'd take it right now if she could only get over the fear that gaining this new side of her might somehow destroy everything she'd worked so hard to achieve.

And walking into John's office with only some scribblings on a pad of paper wasn't helping at all.

"I'm sorry," she said, stepping into his office and taking a seat at his desk. "I didn't get a chance to put together my formal report before our meeting."

She passed over the notes she did have as John smiled and shrugged. "No problem. That's what this meeting is for."

Some of her angst dissipated with the easy smile on his face. Maybe this meeting wouldn't be the disaster she feared.

"Here are the preliminaries on the year-end results," she began, then went on to discuss the highlights and other points of interest. For the next hour, they pored over the report together, calling in staff members as needed to explain some of the numbers. And when they were done, she was left with a long list of tasks to delegate and an overwhelming sense of relief.

The meeting had gone off fine. Not much different than it would have had she spent her weekend analyzing the data alone and drafting a formal report, though she still believed it was always better to do more than less. After all, she hadn't climbed the ladder all the way to chief financial officer by barely skating by.

"So did you enjoy the party Friday night?" John asked as he set the report on top of a pile of papers.

"Yes, I enjoyed it very much."

The man grinned. "I noticed Kit Baldwin managed to get you out on the dance floor."

Her cheeks warmed. "He's…very coercive."

"I was happy to see it. Employees like to see management relax and have fun. It makes us feel approachable, as we should be."

"Absolutely."

"I looked for the two of you after the dance, but you'd disappeared."

She fluttered her eyelashes, not entirely comfortable with where this conversation was going, but before she could work up a response, John laughed casually. "I'm not trying to pry. I know how private you are when it comes to your personal life."

"I—I don't mean to be."

"It's only that Kit seemed pretty interested in you Friday, and I wanted to offer my endorsement. He's a fine man. I've known him for a number of years." He shrugged and added, "I could actually see the two of you hitting it off quite well."

"We did," she blurted, not realizing until after the words flew from her mouth how revealing the statement might be.

"That's great. I'm glad you enjoyed his company." His smile turned and he shifted in his seat. "To be honest, I've been a little worried about you lately."

"Worried?" It was the last thing she'd expected him to say.

"You're a tireless worker," he said. "You give this company two hundred percent when I only ask for one. Not that I don't appreciate the effort. But I've been in this business long enough to recognize someone on the road to burnout. I don't want to lose the best financial officer this company's had during my tenure."

She blinked. "I can assure you I'm very happy here."

"I'd like you to stay that way."

She sat and awkwardly stared at her boss, having no idea what to say. Never would she have imagined being faulted for doing too much. It wasn't part of her vocabulary— wasn't part of her family's values. The way she was raised, perfection was merely average. It was only acceptable to be the best. In fact, as an executive she continually struggled to have more realistic expectations of her staff, not wanting to be the slave driver she knew some people considered her. But never did she expect she'd be asked to lower the bar on herself.

"I'm only trying to express that I was happy to see you relax somewhat on Friday night. It's good for your image. It's good for the spirit. That makes it good for the company." John sheepishly smiled. "And I admit I'm rooting a little for you and Kit. I think you two would be good for each other." He raised a quick hand. "Not that it's any of my business, I know."

Her eyes froze on her boss, not certain that she was really hearing this. Was he actually encouraging her to date Kit?

Somewhere through the fog of disbelief, she heard herself utter, "I fear if things go badly, he'll pull his account with Stryker."

The words shouldn't have come out of her mouth. It revealed more about her dealings with Kit than she felt was prudent at this point. But a side of her felt desperate to clear her conscience when it came to their business relationship. John was right. She and Kit *were* good. So good that she'd spent half of last night asking herself if she'd be willing to resign her position here if it meant she could keep him.

She'd rather not. She wanted them both.

John casually shook his head. "I wouldn't worry about that."

"But what if he did?"

As her heart raced, his expression sobered. "Then I'll lose an account but still have the sharpest financial officer in the industry. Monica, I'm more concerned with you overworking yourself than an account we have on the books. Business comes and goes. Good employees, I need to keep."

"I appreciate you saying that," she said.

She rose from the desk and gathered her things, still a bit stunned but slowly absorbing what she'd just heard. John was right. All work and no play made Monica a dull gal. What she hadn't understood was that it was also hurting her professionally, isolating her from a staff that had homes and families, who made mistakes and asked for concessions. Over the years she'd tried hard to accept that she had unrealistic expectations and it had always been a struggle. What if the answer was as simple as accepting some limitations of her own?

Could the personal life she feared improve her career instead of destroy it?

As she left John's office and entered her own, a thrilling sense of relief came over her—not to mention irony. What were the odds that John would have this conversation with her right as she was struggling with the very issue? It must be life's way of taking care of itself when a person reached a crossroads, and as she continued to reflect on their discussion, she dropped her planner on her desk and out slid a miniature candy cane wrapped in cellophane. It was the one she'd received from that odd Santa Claus Friday night at the party. She'd forgotten all about him.

I can bring a little of Florida to you.

The man certainly had, hadn't he? And as she considered that night, she couldn't help but wonder if there really was such a thing as holiday magic. It definitely felt like a Christmas miracle had found her.

Brushing it off as silly, she moved to toss the candy in the trash, but something stopped her. A sentimental streak, maybe? The superstitious belief that the little candy might be a good luck charm, perhaps? Either way, she opened her desk drawer and tucked it away for safe keeping. Magic or not, that odd Santa had brought her more than Florida. He'd brought her a whole new life.

And intent to grab hold of it, she picked up the phone, called Kit and changed the plans they'd made for this evening. Instead of dinner at a restaurant, she wanted something more intimate. And when the arrangements were made, she did something she hadn't done in as long as she could remember.

She took the afternoon off.

KIT CHECKED THE LOOK on Monica's face as she opened the door to her apartment, wondering whether her change in dinner plans was a good thing or bad. After getting her call, he figured her suggestion to dine at her place meant she either wanted him all to herself—a good thing—or she wanted to deliver her Dear John speech in private— very bad.

He knew she had reservations about their relationship. Despite his assurances to the contrary, she was still uncomfortable with him being a client of her firm, and he didn't doubt that she'd used her day at the office today to gain a clearer perspective. But had that worked for him or against him?

Early indications looked good, judging by the bright smile and the sexy low-slung blouse she wore. Green and silky, it draped loosely over a pair of black nylon slacks that looked easy to slip out of. A pair of simple black sandals exposed red painted toenails, and as he stepped through the door, he decided the ensemble was definitely more suited to celebrating than delivering sorry news.

He whipped a small box of chocolate truffles out from behind his back. "A hostess gift."

Her smile widened. "From a guest who knows the one thing I like better than wine."

He took her in his arms. "There are a number of things you like better than wine, and I know all of them."

Drawing her in for a kiss, he was greeted with something new. Her touch was still tender and responsive, but underneath it something had changed. There was an eagerness that hadn't been there before, a blend of certainty and calm laced with an extra dose of affection. He liked it a lot, and as he kicked the door closed behind him, he speculated that tonight might end up bringing him the outcome he'd hoped.

"I made dinner," she said when they finally came up for air. "Come in." Taking his hand, she led him to the kitchen and offered him a beer. "I've got chicken parmesan in the oven and salads in the fridge, some crusty French bread and a bottle of cabernet."

He raised a brow. "You cooked?"

She opened her mouth to answer, but instead of agreeing, she stood for a moment with a silly gaping grin on her face. Then she finally sighed and admitted, "No. I ordered it from my favorite Italian restaurant down the block." Her shoulders sagged. "I guess I should admit that I can't cook to save my life. I burn toast. About the most I can manage is instant oatmeal."

She moved to the dining table that had been set with white linens, festive china and flowers all arranged so perfectly it looked like the cover of a home decorating magazine. "I did set the table, though, all by myself. I figured if we're going to try our hand at a relationship, I should demonstrate that I can be domestic when called upon. I can't whip up a meal, but I could fake it pretty good if you ever needed me to."

He smiled as the space in his chest warmed. "You don't need to. I like you just the way you are." Then he put his beer down and moved close, hoping his ears hadn't deceived him. "Tell me more about this relationship thing."

Looking up at him with serious eyes, she placed her slim hands on his chest and grazed them over his beating heart. "I think this weekend I might have fallen for a tall handsome cowboy."

"Would that be the same cowboy who's already fallen for you?"

"That's him. I'm not sure how we'll make a long-distance relationship work, but I'd love to give it a try."

"So you've stopped worrying about my relationship with Stryker."

A warm smile brightened her face, revealing that smooth sense of assuredness he'd sensed in the kiss. "I've stopped worrying about a lot of things. What I want to do now is enjoy life a little more while exploring this incredible thing we've got going."

The words were a song to his heart. Cupping her face, Kit brought his mouth to hers and tasted the sweetness of a romance he couldn't wait to dig into. He caressed the smooth skin under his fingertips, soaked in the flowery scent of spring and sunshine and pressed his body against those long slim curves that fit against him just right. He'd known since the first time he touched her that this woman was the one he wanted to keep, and as he slid his hands down her waist and felt the flames burn deep a sense of joy filled him.

"You mentioned something about Christmas," she muttered against his lips.

He pulled back. "You've changed your mind?"

She nodded. "I'd love to see your niece's reaction when she sees the furniture we worked so hard on."

He eyed her quizzically. "You're sure?"

"Yes, but I've got a request." She patted his arm and cleared her throat. "I've got to be in Connecticut Wednesday night at the latest. My mother will never forgive me if I miss the family photo. After that, they're throwing a big Christmas party Friday night and I was hoping you could join me."

"I wouldn't miss it." He noted the nerves in her gaze and asked, "You're really okay missing Christmas with your family?"

She laughed. "My mother will throw a fit. She'll claim I've ruined everyone's holiday, and I'm not looking forward to breaking the news. But at some point, she has to accept the fact that her children are grown adults who are building new families of their own. She needs to learn to bend a little." Then she cradled his face in her palms and added, "Just like I do."

"Sweetheart, I think you're damn near perfect the way you are."

"But I'm better when I'm with you." She pressed her mouth to his and offered him the best Christmas present a guy could ask for. It was a kiss that hardened his body and softened his heart all in one, turning him hot and greedy and needing much more.

"This dinner of yours," he said, sliding his hands up under her blouse. "How long will it keep?"

"Hours I'm sure."

Spoken like a woman who hadn't a clue about cooking. But it only made him smile. They *were* perfect together, strengths and weaknesses combined, and he didn't doubt that together they would both be better than either one of them were apart. And as he tugged her toward the bedroom, he knew without a doubt that this holiday season had brought him a gift he'd cherish forever.

"Then let's put the meal on hold and go create some Christmas traditions of our own."

Sleigh Ride

1

NICK CASTLE WAS listening intently to a debate about this year's Super Bowl prospects when John Stryker Jr. strode up and clapped him on the back. "Another year, another trip to Maui," John said. "Congratulations on the top sales award."

Nick grinned and stepped away from the group. "Thanks, John."

"I don't know how you do it. Everyone had their money on Daryl this year after he hit it big with Jackson Pharmaceuticals."

"Not big enough, I guess." Nick spared a glance at Daryl, who was across the room and still looking bent over losing the award, but those were the breaks. Nick had worked his ass off this year—like he did every year. Anyone hoping to knock him out of first place would have to do better than score one major account.

"In my opinion, you deserved it anyway. You work harder."

"I do."

Nick wasn't at all dismissive of the long hours he put into his job even though he enjoyed them. Scanning the room, he took in the array of high-priced suits and designer dresses. This was a far cry from the dusty Detroit suburb where his father worked on an assembly line and his mother served lunches at the high school. Where Nick came from, folks didn't drive Beemers or wear gold on their wrists. And while he'd never disrespect his parents by being ashamed of his roots, he'd spent a lifetime trying to escape it. Now he was settled comfortably on the other side of the tracks and thrilled to be here.

"To me it's not work," he admitted. "When you love what you do it's like playtime."

The pleasant look on John's face faded. "Must be nice."

Nick regarded him curiously. *Must be nice?* John Jr. was one retirement party from owning the whole damn company. He was filthy rich and had the world by the balls. Nick couldn't fathom a life much better than being born the son of the Chairman. Yet there was John, slugging his beer and surveying his future empire as if he were facing a life sentence at Marion State Prison.

"Dude, it doesn't get *nicer* than being John Stryker Jr."

John shrugged and sighed like only a man who'd never been dirt poor could. "White-collar work has never interested me."

"So what? You're rolling in dough."

"There's more to life than money."

Nick laughed. "Says the guy who's always had it." He pointed a finger at John's chest. "Take it from the one who didn't. Money can buy a lot of happiness. Anyone who says otherwise didn't grow up on my street."

That brought the smile back to John's face. Nodding in agreement, he held his beer up to toast. "All right. I suppose I can't argue with that."

As "Jingle Bell Rock" wafted over the dance floor the

two men stood and watched the festivities. "So who are you taking to Maui this year?" John asked.

Nick considered the question. So far he'd always given the trips to his parents. If anyone deserved a slice of easy street it was Bob and Grace Castle, and Nick made sure that plenty of his good fortune got passed their way. But now they had his elderly grandmother living with them, and he knew that they wouldn't leave the woman for a week on a sandy beach. This year, Nick would be taking the trip himself, and until John mentioned it, he hadn't given half a thought as to whom he'd bring along.

"I've got no idea."

"What about the woman you're dating?"

"Pam? That ended ages ago."

John looked taken aback. "I'm sorry. I didn't know."

Nick shrugged. "Don't be. It was fun for a minute but there was nothing lasting there."

His fascination with the restaurant hostess had been her beauty. That and a pair of legs he couldn't seem to pull his eyes from. But like the half-dozen women before her, their relationship had been superficial. Dating beautiful women had been a schoolboy's test of success that Nick was quickly maturing out of. Now he ached for something real, a connection of body *and* soul. But finding that special someone was much easier said than done. Once he'd raised the bar above a woman merely having a pretty face, the dating world got a whole lot harder. So hard that it had been months since he'd so much as gotten laid.

Thus, all the time he had available for pouring that excess energy into his job.

He smiled at the irony. A vacant love life had helped him inch out the top sales award in an especially tough year, and his reward was a vacation he had no one to share with.

"What about you?" he asked, thinking maybe a bachelor's trip might make a decent consolation.

"Me what?" John asked absently.

"Maui, you and me and whatever island babes we meet along the way."

"Island...right." John's voice drifted off and Nick glanced at the man to discover he was no longer listening to the conversation. John's attention had been thoroughly diverted to someone or something across the room. Following his gaze, Nick found a pretty brunette standing near the buffet watching the dance floor and joyfully tapping her toe to the music.

"Do you know her?" John asked.

"The woman in the pale blue blouse?"

"Yeah."

Nick shook his head. "Never seen her before. You?"

"No," John said wistfully as though the mere sight of her had sent him into a lusty trance.

He tapped Nick on the arm as he began to step away. "Let me catch up with you later." And before Nick could even respond, the man was making a beeline to the mystery girl.

He watched the two converse, both full of laughs and bright smiles, and when they set down their drinks and headed for the dance floor, Nick knew he wouldn't be seeing John again that evening.

Great. How nice of the guy to bring up Nick's empty sex life before leaving him to go chase down a hottie.

With a newfound sense of lacking, he sipped his drink and ignored all that was good in his life to focus on the one thing missing—someone to share it with. He'd only been half joking when he told John that money could buy happiness—half joking because life was a hell of a lot more fun with it than without. But he also knew that not every joy could be bought with dollar bills. And true love and family topped that list.

"Ho, ho, ho!"

Nick turned toward the sound of the laughter to find an old guy in a bright red Santa suit holding his belly and smiling with glee.

Nick quirked a brow. "Enjoying the Christmas cheer tonight?" He sniffed the red-faced man for alcohol but only came up with cinnamon.

"It's a festive time of year, it is," the man agreed.

Nick fingered the sleeve of the guy's red silk suit. "Hey, this is nice stuff. The economy up north must be booming. Who handles your insurance?"

The old man's eyes sparkled. "My insurance is the joy I bring to people around the world. The sound of a child's laughter is my treasure."

"Right." Nick nodded, deciding pretty quickly that the guy was a fruitcake. "So what are you doing here, Claus? Making a list? Checking it twice? I've been a little naughty *and* nice. What'll that get me?"

Claus pulled a miniature candy cane from his pocket and handed it to Nick.

"Not much, eh," Nick said, accepting the token.

"You need to tell me what you want first. Then we'll see what I can do."

"That's the way it goes, huh?"

Nick eyed the odd guy, figuring he was most likely hired entertainment, a poor schmuck just doing his job, and as Nick looked him over, he figured Claus had pulled off a pretty decent rendition of old St. Nick. The guy definitely beat out the half-crocked hobo ringing bells down on the corner. So in the spirit of the season and wanting to cut the man a break, he gave the question a moment's thought.

What *did* he want for Christmas? For a guy with

everything it wasn't a simple question. But while he pondered, the music shifted to "White Christmas" and those couples still on the dance floor moved close and began a sultry sway. He saw John and the mystery woman pawing over each other as though life beyond their three-foot square of the dance floor had ceased to exist, and a spark of envy came over him.

That was what he wanted. He'd achieved success in every other aspect of his life, but still needed the one thing that remained elusive.

"Give me the girl of my dreams, Claus. My soul mate. My happily ever after."

Without so much as twitching a white bushy eyebrow, Claus replied, "That's easy. She's in the ladies' room."

Now it was Nick's turn to laugh. *"In the bathroom?"*

"Yes, and you'll want to hurry if you intend on catching her."

Through the chuckles he realized the guy wasn't joking. "Why don't you just tell me who it is and I'll give her a call in the morning?"

Claus shook his head and grinned. "Now, that wouldn't be fun. Why, it would be like handing out gifts without wrapping them first."

"Right." Nick pointed to the doorway. "But if I run down the hall, I'll find her in the john."

"I'd recommend you wait for her to come out."

Nick shook his head and laughed some more, certain this guy was a whack-job and now wondering if he'd even been hired for the party. On second thought, maybe he was—hired by Jeannie but recruited by his coworkers to pull off a practical joke. Heck, maybe Daryl was behind this, hoping to get Nick good for stealing top honors tonight.

As he eyed the room for onlookers, he decided that had

to be it. Only when he turned to tell Claus that he was onto them, the jolly guy was gone.

"Hurry!" Nick heard over his shoulder and he swung around only to find the group by the bar still arguing over sports and oblivious to anything beyond them.

He swung left then right, scanning every corner of the ballroom but there was no sign of the white-haired man in the red silk suit. Now, that was weird. But it still wasn't odd enough to convince Nick that this was more than a practical joke or a bearded screwball loose in the building.

He shrugged the whole thing off. Either way, he wasn't going to play into the ruse. He polished off the last of his drink and headed to the bar for another, determined to put the whole thing behind him. The only problem was curiosity kept needling him, urging him to go out there and see what awaited him down the hall. Despite the certainty that he'd show up at the restrooms as the brunt of a big fat joke, he couldn't help but wonder.

What if it wasn't a joke? What if he had a secret admirer who'd gone through the trouble to set all this up? Maybe his dream girl really was out there and had planned an elaborate scheme to make her feelings known.

Then he remembered that the Christmas wish had been *his* idea. He was the one who'd asked for a soul mate. If he'd asked for a Ferrari would the guy have still sent him down the hall?

The more he weighed it, the more his conspiracy theory was thinning.

Which meant Santa was a nutcase and Nick needed to forget about it.

Determined to brush off the encounter, he continued toward the bar, but the second his feet went into motion he started toward the restrooms instead. Damn if he couldn't get the stupid curiosity out of his head, and knowing that time was ticking away, he didn't have the luxury to keep debating his options. Fruitcake or not, Nick had to go see if someone was really there. Maybe it would be no one. Maybe it would be Agnes, the sixty-seven-year-old accounting supervisor who just celebrated her fiftieth wedding anniversary. Or maybe it would be Daryl ready to point a finger and laugh over the fact that Nick might have taken the sales award, but he was still a royal stooge.

The more the seconds ticked by the more he had to know. He pushed his way through the big double doors, stepped into the quiet of the hallway and made his way down the corridor. When he reached the restroom door, he resisted the urge to barge inside and instead waited. He heard the sound of running water. Someone was in there, and the knowledge had him suddenly feeling ridiculous. What was he doing loitering in front of the women's bathroom because some quack in a Santa suit said his dream girl was inside? Was it a sign of gullibility or desperation? Both were good indicators that Nick needed professional help for the simple fact that he was actually standing there waiting for the woman to come out. This was dumb. More than dumb. It was insanity. And in a last-ditch effort to prove himself of sound mind, he turned and started to go back to the party.

Right then, the door clicked open behind him. As he turned back, he caught a glimpse of the woman who Claus claimed was his soul mate. Then he started to laugh. Hard. Not a nervous laugh, or a friendly one, or the giddy chuckles of relief. It was a wild, guttural cackle that bordered on hysteria.

His first instinct was most definitely correct. This was a practical joke, and whoever came up with it deserved a pat on the back for a job well done. Because if this was a joke, they knew exactly the right woman to place in the bathroom for the best ever punch line.

Stryker & Associates employed upward of 300 people, and 299 of them would say that Nick Castle was a pretty good guy. He was well liked by everyone—even Daryl, who despite their competitive natures, still considered Nick a friend. There was only one person who, due to a series of unfortunate incidents—*twelve fricking months ago*— deeply and wholeheartedly hated his guts. That person was his fellow sales agent Allie Madison.

As he stood there guffawing like an idiot, Allie looked up and frowned. "Had a few too many cocktails tonight, Nick?"

It only made him laugh harder, but then a thought stopped him cold. "Hey, is anyone else in the women's restroom?"

Her frown turned to bland amusement. "What happened? Did your girlfriend ditch you?"

"Just answer the question, Allie."

She glanced back at the door then at him. "You're right. Whatever's going on, I probably don't want to know." She started down the hall and back toward the party swinging those sexy damnable hips as she went. Flipping her silky blond hair over one shoulder, she said, "It's empty. The room's all yours." Then she tossed him a look that actually brought a flush of embarrassment to his cheeks.

He opened his mouth to stop her then quickly snapped it shut. What would he say? *It's not how it looks. I'm only here because that guy dressed as Santa told me I'd find my soul mate in the can?*

That would clear things up swimmingly. Then, not only could she rue the ground he walked on, but she could also claim him certifiable, too. So he pressed his lips into a disgruntled line, and did what he should have done in the first place. He went back to the party and tried to forget the whole thing.

2

ALLIE MADISON ENTERED the ballroom angry with herself that after all this time she still couldn't come close to Nick Castle without salivating. What was wrong with her? Was her memory so short and her values so shallow that she could simply erase history for a charming smile and handsome face?

She crossed to the bar and ordered a vodka cranberry, hoping maybe a drink would wipe Nick's sinful good looks from her thoughts. It wasn't right that a man should be graced with such an overwhelming combination of bottomless blue eyes, black tousled hair and sharp sexy features, then have the personality of a spoiled child. It was a cruel form of punishment, one she'd endured for far too long.

And just now she'd nearly blown it. In the middle of all the celebration and joy she'd nearly forgotten herself when she'd stepped out of the bathroom and caught the sizzle of his gaze meeting hers. Her knee-jerk reaction had been to smile brightly and offer an eager hello. Fortunately, she'd stopped herself in time. As it went, her perky greeting would have only humiliated her when he'd burst out laughing, and it was another reminder that she was doing the right thing by holding on to her animosity.

Though it would be a lot easier to do if he wasn't so deadly gorgeous. And funny. And oddly well-liked by seemingly everyone but her. If it weren't for those minor details, she would still be enjoying the party instead of standing at the bar slugging down vodka and trying to forget he ever existed.

Her gaze darted to the doorway when she saw Nick step inside, and just like her, his first angle was a direct beeline to the bar. Then his eyes came in contact with hers. Immediately, that luscious mouth of his flattened, giving her a pang of hurt she tried not to acknowledge. Instead, she forced herself to casually turn away, dismissing his presence with a dose of well-practiced disinterest.

Jeannie Carmichael stepped within earshot, and Allie struck up a conversation to avoid being caught standing alone like a boob with Nick approaching.

"Hi, Jeannie. Are you enjoying the party?"

The young woman paused on her way to the buffet. "Sure." She let out an exasperated breath. "It's a big job organizing it, though. A lot more work than I'd expected."

"That's right. You're the one who got stuck with it this year after they laid off Carla."

Jeannie nodded then added cheerfully, "As long as everyone's enjoying themselves, it's worth it, I guess."

Allie gave her a thumbs-up. "That's the corporate spirit."

Out of the corner of her eye, she saw Nick join a group of men who'd been circled near the other end of the bar for most of the evening. As Nick approached them he said something that caused them all to roar with laughter.

Grinding her teeth, she turned back to Jeannie and tried to focus as the woman went on about the party arrangements, but then a second roar of laughter tugged her back. As much as Allie tried to concentrate on her coworker, she couldn't shake Nick's presence only a few yards away. That low voice of his slid like a caress down her spine, his easy chuckle tingled across her skin, and each time she caught sight of him with his trim waist and tight butt a trickle of warmth settled between her thighs and made her squirm.

Oh, she had it bad. So many late-night fantasies had starred that man she ought to pay him royalties. But in her dreams he wasn't just a handsome face and sexy body. The orgasmic version of Nick Castle was also thoughtful and kind. He cared as much about Allie as he did for himself. And most importantly, in her dreams, he actually liked her. He thought she was fun and interesting, smart and capable, and the ache in his heart for her matched her ache for him.

Totally lame, of course, because she knew none of it was true. But heaven help the fact that she couldn't connect her body to her brain and stop the confounded lust no matter how hard she tried.

"Anyway, I guess I'm boring you with all these stupid details," Jeannie remarked, yanking Allie back to their conversation.

"Oh, I'm sorry," Allie said. "I really am interested in hearing about everything you've done." Though even as she said the words, half an eye crept back to Nick and his friends.

Had one of them uttered her name?

Jeannie followed Allie's gaze. "That's okay. Nick has that effect on all the women."

That snapped Allie to attention. "No! It's not Nick. Nick Castle?" Involuntarily, she chuckled in a high-pitched shrilly kind of way. "That's not it at all. I just thought—I mean, he's a big nothing, a zero, a…"

Allie noted that she was grossly overplaying her hand. Quickly, she took a breath and tried to get it back together.

"I'm sorry. You were talking and I missed what you'd said. That was rude. Please, go on."

Jeannie shrugged and smiled, though her eyes hinted of a disappointment that made Allie feel like a heel. "Don't worry about it." Jeannie gestured toward the buffet. "I've actually got to tend to a few things, so maybe I'll catch up with you after a while." Then she turned and crossed the room.

Great, Allie. That was really nice. Not only did she succeed in insulting a sweet girl who deserved better, but Allie had also left herself alone once again.

She scanned the room in search of a place to go and spotted Mike Holden chatting with a man she recognized from IT. Now, there was a guy she should be focusing her attention on. Mike was friendly and considerate, and quite successful in his little corner of Operations. He wasn't bad to look at and had even asked her on a date once, though she'd turned him down. At the time, she'd just come off her disastrous relationship and had promised herself she'd take a break from men to get her head on straight. Instead, she'd spent the next year lusting over Nick Castle, even after he'd pulled the stunt that proved him completely unworthy.

Since then, she hadn't given Mike a second glance, but maybe it was time to start exploring her options. Sure, there were no sparks with Mike, but wasn't she supposed to start running her love life with her brains instead of those unreliable hormones of hers?

Yes, she was. And as a Christmas gift to herself she decided to do just that. So with the sexy murmur of Nick's deep voice still echoing down her spine, she dropped her glass at the bar and set off to see if Mike's proposal was still on the table after all this time.

"HEY, HAVE ANY OF YOU talked to that weird Santa Claus working the room?" Nick asked his group of coworkers.

"What Santa?" asked Dale, a senior accountant in Finance.

Nick eyed the room intending to point the man out, but the odd Claus was nowhere to be found. "The guy in the red suit handing out candy canes."

The men looked at each other. "I don't know what you're talking about," said Myles, an analyst in underwriting.

Nick studied his friends, getting from their expressions they weren't pulling his leg. Apparently, none of them had seen him.

"Then the old man really *was* a whack-job." Nick gestured to Jeannie, who was standing at the other end of the bar chatting with Allie. "Jeannie must have had the guy thrown out."

"What did he do, try to sell you some magic reindeer dust?" Myles asked, prompting laughs from the group.

"Even weirder." Nick told them about his encounter with Claus and the dream girl he was supposed to find in the bathroom. Immediately, the jokes started flying.

"Damn, I've been looking for my soul mate. Maybe I should check the utility closet," Dale teased.

"Yeah," added Cliff. "I'm seeing a new version of that TV dating show. 'So what's your choice, Nick, stall number one, stall number two or stall number three?'"

The men roared, but Nick wasn't nearly as amused. In retrospect, he should have known better than to share the harebrained story. What was he thinking? Knowing these guys, he'd be hearing about this for years.

Intent to play it like a good sport, he stood and silently brooded while the comedians came up with more jokes. In some way this had to be Allie's fault, he thought, as he gazed at the sultry blonde from the corner of his eye. If anyone else had walked out of that bathroom, odds were he'd have dismissed the whole thing without a second thought. But of all people, it had to have been her, the one woman in the *entire building* who could get him steamed, hot, aroused and furious all with one cutting remark and a flip of that silky blond hair.

No one had the ability to slither under his skin with such efficiency, and no one used that talent as enthusiastically as Allie Madison. She hated him with a passion, despite his numerous efforts to apologize for the incident that had turned her against him. No matter what he'd tried, she'd labeled him pond scum for life, and for reasons he might never understand, that bugged the hell out of him.

While his friends continued to clown at his expense, he watched as Allie sauntered off, her perfect heart-shaped ass looking exceptionally festive in that green silk skirt. What a waste of a beautiful body, all those luscious curves and bends. She had eyes the color of dark chocolate, a sexy mole just above her full red lips and smooth satin hair he could practically feel slipping sensually through his fingers. There was so much potential wrapped up in that pretty package, it was a shame to know there was nothing but coal inside. Things could have been so different.

"You went and looked, didn't you?"

Nick blinked back to the group, only now noticing the four men had stopped chatting and were watching him intently, waiting for him to answer the question.

"Huh?"

"The bathroom," Cliff said. "Ten bucks says you actually walked down the hall to see who was there."

"I..." Nick bobbed his jaw, undecided on how to answer, but apparently the look on his face answered for him.

"Dude, you did!"

"Who was there?" asked Dale.

"It was Tracy in Accounting," Myles guessed.

"No, my bet's on Debbie Swanson."

Nick fumbled as the men continued to rattle off every available woman in the company. But it was Tom Wilcox, who'd been quiet up to this point, who blurted out with too much intuition in his tone, "It was Allie Madison."

Nick's gaze collided with Tom's.

Logically, this would be the point where the real jokes began, the ones Nick could get in on because the idea of Allie as his dream girl was the best one of all. Only no one was laughing. Instead, his band of comics was standing there eyeing each other like someone had just dropped a fly in his soup.

"Yes, it was Allie," he said, studying each of them and wondering why the mood had suddenly turned.

Cliff raised a brow. "So what are you going to do about it?"

Nick scoffed. "*Do?* I'm going to write it off as a Christmas fruitcake. *That's* what I'm going to do."

Cliff slid a glance at Dale.

"*What?*" Nick urged. "What happened to the jabs? Where's the jokes about how ridiculous this is? You know you've got them." He waved his hands in invitation. "Bring them on. I can take it."

He waited while the men stood fidgeting like a gang of guilty schoolboys until Tom finally said, "C'mon, Nick. We all know she's your one major heartbreak. We wouldn't joke about that."

"The one that got away," Dale chimed in.

Nick gaped. "You're kidding, right? *Allie,* my heartbreak? That's insane."

He began laughing in that same maniacal tone that had erupted back at the bathrooms. Oh, this night was weird and getting weirder by the moment. First the quack-nut

Santa, then Allie in the hall, and now this? Something odd was happening to him tonight. So odd that he half expected Rod Serling to step in and introduce him to *The Twilight Zone*.

Myles held up his hands. "Hey, if that's how you want to play it, who are we to argue?"

"Yeah," Cliff agreed, and the other two nodded in that patronizing way one might address a temperamental child—or an unstable cousin who was one prescription away from the psych ward.

"I'm serious," Nick defended. "I've never carried a torch for that woman."

Though even he felt a twinge of falsehood in that statement. Okay, so maybe once long ago he'd been hung up on Allie. But that was early on and had been entirely squelched when he got to know her. After the Halpin Technologies fiasco, he'd seen her dark side and it pretty much iced any heat he might have felt for the woman. Now, he spent most of his energy avoiding her like the plague.

"I'm serious," he insisted. "A gallon of spiked eggnog couldn't prompt my interest in that walking nutcracker."

"Okay, Nick. We believe you," Cliff said in a tone that said he didn't.

"Right."

For a long awkward minute they all stood and stared until Tom finally cleared his throat and asked, "Anyone got the line on the Bulls game?"

And that easily, the conversation moved on to sports and holiday plans and everything other than Nick's love life. But by then it was too late. He was officially bugged, out of holiday spirit and in need of someone to reassure him that everyone hadn't gone mad.

The one that got away. What kind of cockamamie notion was that? "Look, I'll catch up with you guys later," he said. Then he took off in search of more logical minds. Those guys had chugged down one too many cocktails tonight, was all. Surely, if Nick shared his experience with someone more sober, he'd get the reaction he'd expected.

He caught up with Jodi, one of the analysts known for having a pulse on just about everything. When he relayed the gist of his evening, she smiled brightly and exclaimed, "I always thought you and Allie would be perfect for each other."

That sent him on to Timmy La, a web programmer he'd known for years.

"I thought you two were already dating," Tim said.

He abandoned Tim for Peter Newcome.

"Crap, I would have hit on her ages ago, but I assumed it would piss you off," Pete said.

"Why the hell would I care?"

Pete shrugged. "Well, you know."

No, Nick didn't, but after tracking down three more opinions, he was getting the picture. It seemed everyone in this place assumed he was either a lover scorned or still pining over the woman he couldn't have. It was nuts, pure and simple, but apparently the opinion almost everyone shared. And if he had half a brain he'd chalk it all up to either too much alcohol or one big practical joke. But he didn't have half a brain. What he had was the stubborn will to keep searching until someone in this room provided a voice of reason.

And unfortunately, he knew there was only one person here certain to see things his way. So with no other options, he went off in search of Allie.

3

Nick found Allie at an out-of-the-way table holding a cozy conversation with Mike Holden.

A bit too cozy for your liking.

He clenched his teeth and batted off that stupid thought. See? This was the problem with soliciting opinions from a group of sentimental coworkers. They put silly thoughts in his head that had no basis in reality.

The thoughts were already there and you know it.

He ground his teeth. Okay, maybe they were. But that was ages ago before she'd made it clear she wanted nothing to do with him. Since then, he'd gotten over her. Way over her. He'd buried those early desires, had moved on with his life without ever giving the woman another steamy sexual thought.

You mean other than the three times a day you happen to see her in the halls?

The stupid voice was making him cranky, and rather than spend the night arguing with it, he stepped up to the table and blurted, "Allie, I need to talk to you." He eyed Mike and added, "Alone."

Allie huffed. "And just when I thought you couldn't get any more boorish."

Her comment stung, especially since he knew it was true, but he excused his abruptness on grounds that he wasn't exactly himself right then. This place had gotten him worked up, and on occasions when he felt threatened, the gritty kid from Detroit usually did the talking.

"It's okay. I don't mind." Mike rose from the table in his nice-guy, accommodating way, but Allie grabbed his hand.

"*I* do." She eyed Nick with a glint of challenge in her eye. "Mike and I were having a private conversation and you've interrupted. Despite how it seems, everyone in this place doesn't scramble just because you want something."

Though she kept a straight face, he could see the joy seep through those fudge-colored eyes. He needed her and she got to say no. It was probably something she'd waited months for.

Regardless, he tried again, speaking slowly to maintain his calm. "I'm sorry to interrupt, but if I could have a word with Allie in private, I would very much appreciate it." He gave his best salesman smile. "I promise it won't take long."

"I'll go get us a couple drinks," Mike said, now clearly anxious to get out from between them.

"Thanks, pal. I'll be out of your hair in a minute."

As Mike walked off, Nick slid into his seat.

"Make it quick, Castle," Allie said, then she grinned. "Mike and I are planning our first date."

An illogical coil of jealousy snaked up his spine, causing him to get straight to the point. "I need you to tell me you're not my soul mate."

That wiped the grin off her face.

"What?"

"It's that stupid Santa," Nick said as he wiped his palms

on his slacks and scanned the room for the man one last time. "He started this whole thing."

Half muttering and half babbling, he shot out his story starting with Santa Claus and the Christmas wish and ending with his and Allie's encounter outside the restrooms.

"So you see why I was laughing," he explained. "*You,* my soul mate? You hate my guts."

He chuckled, feeling surprisingly relieved to finally share the story with Allie, knowing she of all people would understand. And while she did grace him with the scoff he'd been seeking, something was missing from her expression.

Ignoring her look, he plowed on. "I don't know where that guy came from. I can't seem to find anyone who saw him but me."

"You mean the stocky man with the white beard and that weird red silk suit?"

Nick gaped. "You've seen him?"

She nodded, her canned amusement now beginning to fade. "I ran in to him earlier."

"Hallelujah, I thought I was going mad." He leveled his gaze with hers. "Then you know what a fruitcake he is. I mean, telling me I'll find the girl of my dreams in the bathroom. What's up with that?"

She waved him off. "Oh, yeah. Totally out there, for sure."

"So you can imagine the irony when the guy psyches me into walking down the hall and I find *you* there."

"Imagine."

"The idea of you and me…" He trailed off with a roll of laughter.

"Absurd," she offered.

"Yes. Thank you. That's all I needed to hear." He sighed and fell back against his chair, feeling normal and whole once again now that he'd finally gotten this out in the open and cleared the air.

But his relief was short-lived. Though Allie had spoken all the words he'd expected, something about their exchange felt wrong. Fake. False even. Her cheeks had flushed to a bright pink, the rest of her face was pale, and her smile seemed plastic.

"Glad I could help," she said. Abruptly, she rose from the table. "When Mike comes back would you tell him I had to step out for a moment?"

"Sure," he replied, though he doubted she'd heard him. She was gone and out of there before he could say "Merry Christmas." And just like that, all the reassurance he'd sought went up the chimney like old St. Nick.

What had just happened here? Instead of feeling right, this only felt more wrong. More fake. Really false. And as he sat there trying to piece it together, a thought hit him square between the eyes.

Oh, no. No, no, no. That couldn't be it.

He watched as Allie zigzagged through the crowd and fled through the back hall doors with the purpose of someone severely rattled. And he could only figure one reason why their conversation might have struck a bad chord.

That or this night and all these people had succeeded in turning his head in circles.

Either way, he wasn't going to waste another hour trying to figure it out. He'd been doing that half the night and had gotten nowhere. He shoved away from the table and set off after her. It seemed it was time he and Allie had a heart-to-heart, and where it ended, he could only speculate. But no matter what, it was time to get to the bottom of this once and for all.

ALLIE PUSHED THROUGH THE doors to the hallway and sucked in an oversize breath. What a fool she must have looked like back there, bolting up and running out of the room with her face red as a cranberry. Her only consolation was that she would have looked worse had she stayed and let her feelings translate across her face.

It was irrational to be hurt by Nick's comments. Given their history, he didn't say anything she wouldn't have if she'd been in his position. Heck, he was probably nicer. But it still smarted to hear him mock the idea of something romantic between them. Even though she wasn't interested in the man—*and she really wasn't interested*—it had been nice to hold on to the fantasy that somewhere in the dark recesses of his subconscious he might have held a tiny spark of attraction for her. Now, even the fantasy was gone.

She let out a sigh and leaned against the lobby wall, using the muffled clamor of the party to soothe her nerves and collect her thoughts. So Nick had asked Santa for a soul mate. How ironic that she'd asked the man for almost the very same thing. When the jolly guy in red silk had handed her a candy cane and asked what she'd wanted for Christmas she hadn't thought twice. "Mr. Right," she'd said. Then the strange man had given her some anecdote about looking inside her heart.

Apparently, Nick got sent to the ladies' room—which would have had her rolling if it weren't for the heavy weight in her chest.

Down the hall the doors to the party swung open and, not in the mood for conversation, she turned her back and reached into her pockets in an attempt to look busy. Then she heard—make that felt—the low voice behind her.

"I think we need to talk," Nick said.

There was gentleness in his tone that smoothed like lotion over her skin. It was the same voice he used in her dreams. The one she heard in the dark, between the sheets, as his lips and hands seduced her and made her body tingle.

Through much practice, she tamped down her feelings and turned to face him, clipping out a "What about?" as best she could.

She tried not to look as his magnetic blue eyes searched her face and studied her expression, but when their gazes met she couldn't help the feeling that all her secrets were flooding out in front of him.

Still braced against the wall, she pressed her palm to the rough surface and locked her knees. He stood so close she could almost feel the heat of his body pooling over her. Or maybe it was her own betraying reaction to his heady scent and the knowledge that if she only nudged forward a hint her lips would be pressed against the raw stubble of his chin.

"You're upset," he said quietly. "What did I say?"

She swallowed some moisture into her throat and choked out, "I'm not upset."

She diverted her gaze for fear that her face might contradict that statement, but he already saw through it.

"Yes, you are. And I'm responsible. I laughed off the idea of you and me as a couple, but you didn't think it was funny." Touching his warm finger to her jaw, he coaxed her gaze back to his. "Why not, Allie?"

Warning bells began to ring. Nick was speaking softly, touching her, surrounding her space with his unique scent of musk and pine, and her body's response went so deep it scared her. This was Nick, she reminded herself. A man capable of opening her up and then slashing her raw if she didn't protect herself. So she fought to find those shields she always kept handy. Except this time she didn't have the strength to hold them up. Too much sincerity framed his face, mixed with a vulnerability she'd never seen before.

Frantically, she searched for a terse brush-off and came up empty-handed. So instead, she simply uttered, "I don't want to talk about this."

She shrugged off his grasp but her skin still sizzled where he'd held her. How she ached to feel that touch everywhere.

He let out a flustered sigh and leaned against the wall. "I think we need to, but if you aren't ready, I'll go ahead and do the talking." He swallowed. "You know what I really wish more than anything?"

She shook her head.

"I wish I knew how to make you stop hating me."

A heavy pulse struck her chest. Leave it to Nick to get straight to the core of the matter. It was one of the things she both loved and hated about him, and one of the things she had the most trouble dealing with when she didn't feel like facing the truth. But he'd gone and laid a card on the table in what looked like pure sincerity. She supposed she could offer him something in return.

"About Halpin Technologies," she said. "I admit that I overreacted. You didn't deserve that much backlash."

There. She said it. And as the words rolled out, she braced herself for Nick's reply. Surely, he would take the bone and run with it, throwing his head back in laughter and rushing back to the party to announce to everyone that Allie Madison finally admitted that she blew an unfortunate incident into a giant fiasco.

And if he did, she probably deserved it.

Halpin Technologies was an account she'd been assigned when she first started with the company, and being one of her firsts, she'd wanted to make a good impression. So she spent weeks studying the company and planning an updated insurance portfolio. She'd thought she had a good plan, had been proud of her efforts, and when Nick took an interest, she'd laid it out before him in the hope of gaining his praise.

Instead, he'd torn her ideas to pieces. He'd pointed out flaws, had talked around her strategy as if he knew Halpin Technologies better than she did, which was ridiculous. She was the one who'd studied their corporate culture and risk management. So she'd brushed him off and expected that to be the end of it.

Only, it wasn't. When Nick found out that she intended to ignore his advice, he'd shared his concerns with Stryker, who quickly pulled the account from Allie and gave it to Nick. That was the event that started the year-long war between them, and Allie had scorned his very existence ever since.

But time had made her see things more clearly. In her anger and humiliation, it had been easy to ignore the fact that a lot of what Nick had said had been spot-on in the first place. Add to that his reaction to Stryker's move. Nick had fought against it. Right in front of her, he'd argued that she should keep the account, had even praised some of her suggestions, but Stryker had held firm. John had felt that as far as the account went Allie was in over her head given her lack of experience, and only offered to let her and Nick team up as long as Nick remained the lead.

Nick had apologized. He'd backed off, had offered to give the account back, let her do it her way and only act as a front man to Stryker. He'd even offered to give her the full commission, but by then she was already ten steps past compromise. She'd taken his actions as total betrayal and had washed her hands of him and the account. She'd even spent a period of time searching for another job until she'd calmed down and started thinking rationally.

But by then she and Nick had moved into a pattern. They'd started hating each other for the sake of hating each other, even long after she'd come to acknowledge the part she'd played in their demise. Hurt kept fueling more hurt, which prompted more cutting remarks and kept the cycle going.

Until tonight, when the festive music and twinkling lights, Christmas wishes and sparkling air of romance had started wearing her down. Nick wanted her to stop hating him, and heaven help her she wanted that, too. But right now, that fate was in Nick's hands. She'd just offered him an olive branch by admitting that she'd made more out of Halpin Technologies than she should have. Would he accept it with grace or hold it up as a trophy for finally winning their battle of wills?

His blue eyes widened. Clearly, he hadn't expected that admission from her. She watched as he blinked and tried to process the sentiment behind her words, and as he did, something good began to smolder under the surface.

"I've wished a million times that I could take that all back," he said, his voice hoarse and regretful. "I never meant for things to turn out that way."

"You weren't the only one with fault. I should have told you that a long time ago. I'm sorry."

The air thickened, making it hard to breathe. Or maybe it was the swirl of relief, appreciation and heat churning in his eyes. He inched closer, consuming her space and snatching the strength from her limbs. On the surface, it came off as an innocent shift from one foot to the other. But to Allie, he was bringing that sexy body within reach of hands that ached for his touch, of lips that tingled for a taste of his mouth on hers, and of a breast that tightened at the hint of his chest so near.

"I'd give anything for a truce," he whispered.

"I'd like that." *And more.*

His steamy gaze lowered to her lips as though he'd read

her thoughts, and in the freak chance that he could, in her head she yelled, *Kiss me, please. Put those big hands on my breasts and squeeze. Touch me until it hurts and then consume me until I'm spent and weak and drained of all this lust.*

That was what she really needed. Not just shared apologies or a promise to get along. She needed the man in her bed, his body in hers, fulfilling every wet fantasy she'd ever had so that she could move beyond this vulnerable state and function like a human being again.

"You really forgive me," he said.

"Yes, and I really don't hate you."

He nudged closer so that now that sensual mouth was only inches from hers. "And when that Santa Claus suggested you were the girl of my dreams. What should I do with that?"

Her breath was so shallow she was nearly dizzy. With naked intent he studied her, his eyelids heavy, his lips twitching, and his body held so still she could almost feel his heartbeat rapping like sound waves against her breast. And with barely the air to utter the words, she heard herself say, "I think maybe you should kiss me and see what happens."

It was all the invitation he needed.

4

THIS MORNING, IF SOMEONE had told Nick he'd be kissing Allie Madison tonight in the back hallways of the Willis Tower, he would have suggested they see a therapist. The absurdity of it would have been too much to accept. Yet when his lips touched Allie's he felt nothing unusual about it. Instead, it felt right as rain, as if twelve months of animosity had unraveled with one simple kiss. And when it did, the admiration, want and attraction that had started the whole thing came back with complete clarity.

He remembered when she'd first started with the firm and how badly he'd wanted her back then. He'd known in those early weeks that Allie had everything he admired and all the qualities that would make her perfect for him.

And on top of that, she was smoking hot.

From the start, she'd charmed him with her smarts and unabashed will for cutting through the bull. Allie was driven and bright, gracious and kind. She was everything he was but refined, her upper middle-class background leaving her with a more polished finish than his gritty Detroit scrubs. And from the moment he saw her, he knew he had to have her.

But it was those same qualities along with his foolish

impatience that had done them in. Going to Stryker on that damned account had been the dumbest move he could have made. If he'd just taken his time to get to know Allie before rushing in to claim her, he would have known that clear as day. But he hadn't, and when the chips fell, she'd used those very same qualities he adored to tear him into shreds.

So, pained and wounded, he'd retreated, spending the next year trying to brush the woman from his heart with mixed success. Sure, he'd told himself countless times that he was over Allie Madison, but it was pretty obvious right now that it never really happened. This fire between them tonight had swept up too hot, too fast. And now that he had her, he wasn't going to blow the chance again.

Slipping a hand around her waist, he drew her close and relished the perfection in his arms. She tasted like sweet berries, smelled like summer, and her body smoothed so perfectly against his it was as though they were bred to join. So many times he'd ached for this connection, had dreamed and wondered to the point of distraction what it would be like to hold her in his arms. Reality wasn't disappointing him. The soft press of her lips, the firm curve of her waist, the silken caress of her hair against his fingertips—it was exactly as he'd imagined, only better.

Parting her lips in welcome, she tilted her head and accepted him in, coaxing his tongue to hers with light eager strokes. Allie was aggressive in business, never afraid to speak her mind, and now he'd found that trait wasn't limited to premiums and deductibles. As they tangled and kissed she smoothed her hands over his chest, across his hips and down his ass, squeezing and prodding with the determination of a woman who knew exactly what she wanted and wasn't afraid to take it.

And it was one helluva turn-on.

Blood rushed south, making him dizzy. He gripped her waist to keep his bearings and she shuddered and groaned, driving the kiss deeper in response to the touch. *Oh, you like it hard, don't you?* He doubted he'd survive it, at least not this first time around. She felt too good in his arms, had lived too long in his fantasies. If this ended up where he hoped it might, it would be enough not to make a fool of himself in his eagerness to satisfy the year-long yearning.

In one long, smooth stroke, she trailed her fingers up his spine, sending a spray of sparks through his pores, and setting his mind on a quest to move this party somewhere private. He ached to touch those firm breasts in the flesh, slip his hands between her bare thighs and use his tongue in places that would pull her apart.

Dragging his mouth from hers, he nipped at her chin and whispered, "I want more than a kiss."

"Lots more," she agreed. Grabbing hold of his tie, she tugged him closer and whispered in his ear, "How far away is your apartment?" Then she brushed her waist against his erection, as if he needed the extra help.

"Too far." He took her hand and led her toward the elevators. "But I know a place that's close."

ALLIE HAD NO IDEA WHERE Nick was taking her, nor did she care. As long as it was private, she wasn't picky about the accommodations. Besides, there'd been dozens of places in this building where she'd fantasized about having her way with Nick Castle. The file room in Operations, the Skydeck, the women's restroom, the electrical closet; she'd left a mental imprint of her and Nick in just about every room with a door—and several without. And now she was about to play out that fantasy in the flesh.

Was this really happening?

She'd asked Nick to kiss her and he didn't hesitate. Apparently, he was as willing to put the past behind them as she. But for what? Was this a one-time thing? Was she only another conquest? Not only had Nick snagged his share of bombshells—and she'd heard there'd been a few—but with her he could also claim victory in the ultimate challenge: bedding the woman who'd hated him. Wouldn't that be a story for the guys at the bar? And as she and Nick stepped out of the elevator and into Stryker's corporate offices, she wondered how she'd feel when word of this got around.

Then Nick eyed her with those beautiful sizzling blues and the hungry look on his face swiped her mind of everything other than that bone-melting kiss and the need for much more. Her body was on fire. Lust poured through her veins. She'd wanted this for so long, she wasn't about to deny herself the pleasure over fears of what would come on Monday. So, shoving any reservations away, she went with him down the hall and into one of Stryker's executive offices.

"Is it okay to be here?" she asked, looking around the large room that had once been the office of Darnell Paige, an executive who'd recently taken a job in New York.

Nick closed the door and turned the lock. "Until they replace Darnell, I consider this vacant space." Tugging her into his arms, he noted the expression on her face. "Relax. I come here and read all the time. It's a dead zone during office hours. There definitely won't be anyone around here tonight."

He kissed her on the lips and added, "Besides, I can't tell you how many times I've thought about you and me in this room." He kissed her chin. "On that desk." He kissed her neck. "On the couch." He kissed lower and nudged her back two steps. "Up against this wall." Her back met the smooth surface of the dark mahogany paneling, and she melted against it. "In my dreams, I've taken you every possible way in this room."

He'd fantasized about her?

Clasping her waist, he moved his lips close to her ear. "Can I show you some of the things I've imagined?"

He circled his thumbs around her taut nipples and a spray of heat swept through her. "Ohhhh, yes."

He devoured her again, just like he'd done in the hallway, as his fingers went to work unbuttoning her blouse. Bit by bit, the fabric loosened and he pressed his mouth to the sensitive flesh he revealed. Every sultry kiss sizzled, stealing her breath and fluttering her pulse until the blouse fell from her shoulders and pooled at her feet.

He cupped her breasts and groaned. "So many times in my thoughts I've held these in my hands, but they were never as beautiful as this."

His voice was rough and sexy, and when he bent down and gently bit through the lace of her bra, she gasped with delight.

"You like it rough, don't you, babe?"

"I like it all."

He licked a circle between her breasts then bit the other nipple. "Me, too. Sometimes gentle? Sometimes hard?"

"Yes," she hissed.

With quick hands he discarded her bra then he devoured her breasts with the same hungry greed as he'd devoured her mouth. Pain and pleasure mixed as he alternately nipped, kissed and sucked, and she laced her fingers through his dark hair, grasping the nape of his neck and prodding him to do more. Her knees weakened. The cool air felt tight against her hot skin, and the low sound of his pleasured moans swept her toward frenzy.

"I've had fantasies about you, too," she confessed.

"Really." He lowered to his knees and kissed her navel. "And what did I do in your fantasy?"

Lifting her skirt, he pressed his mouth directly between her legs.

"That," she said through a low, guttural moan.

He found the clasp to her skirt and sent it cascading down her legs, leaving her naked of all but her green satin thong and glittery gold heels. She scraped her fingernails against the smooth wall and swallowed hard. Never before had she been so hungry for a man, so thirsty for his touch, and when he pressed his lips high on her thigh she nearly crumbled. If he dared touch her sweet spot she'd be over the edge.

Not wanting to come so soon, she steeled herself against the sensation.

"I have another fantasy where I've got you in my mouth," she said.

He stopped kissing her and coughed. "That's a good fantasy."

"It would make a better reality."

"Remind me to get to that later."

Tucking his fingers in the elastic, he pulled her thong down her thighs and to the floor and her body went on high alert.

"Really," she uttered. "Let's move to the couch so you can get in on this, too."

"I'm in deep already, babe." Then with the determination she should have expected of Nick, he slid close and went straight for her clit.

White heat shot through her when his tongue swept between her folds. Involuntarily, her hips jerked and she let out a high squeak. "You'll make me come," she warned.

"That's where I'm going with this."

"But—ohhhh."

He grasped her thighs and suckled her nub, and with a surge of pure ecstasy, she lost the desire to argue. It felt too good and she'd been thrust too far. Parting her legs, she let him have her. Oh, the man had talent, using just the right amount of pressure in just the right place to draw out those last succulent moments. And just when she neared the peak, he slipped a finger inside and stroked her G-spot, sending her crashing with a force that nearly brought her to her knees.

She tightened her fingers in his hair and held on tight, biting her lips to muffle her cries as the orgasm took control. Through the fog, she heard him groan with indulgence as her pleasure fed his, her release spiking his need and feeding his own satisfaction. It was a sound that warmed her heart as much as it simmered her blood, and before her own climax even subsided, she ached to have him fill her.

Nick rose and took her in his arms, his blue eyes now darkened to midnight, colored with heat and affection and a need she knew rivaled her own. The orgasm was amazing, but more than that, she wanted to connect with this man who'd been stirring her blood since she'd met him.

A smile immediately curved his lips and he wasted no time in picking her up and depositing her on the large executive desk.

"I liked that fantasy you mentioned, but I had another of my own I'd like to get to first."

She eyed the bulge behind his zipper and asked, "Does it involve this desk?"

His smile turned delightfully sinister. "You've got it, babe."

5

NICK STOOD OVER ALLIE, sheathed and hard and ready to slide into her hot, soft core when the simple sight of her gave him pause. The woman was exquisite, lying there naked and vulnerable with her cheeks flushed and lips plump from kissing.

He'd ached for this moment—for this sight—from the very first time she'd walked into Stryker's offices and turned his head. And now after everything they'd been through, he finally had her here in his arms, exposed and willing to take him in the most intimate way. It was nearly too much to handle.

Grasping her hips, he positioned himself and slid in, a glorious liquid heat pouring over him as her velvet core encased him. He groaned and nearly lost his footing as the sensation swept through, the heady combination of physical pleasure and raw emotion that spoke to him deeply and colored his vision.

In his fantasies, this encounter on the desk had been a fun, casual romp. But with new revelations flooding him, he only wanted to close his mouth over hers and claim her with a connection that would brand her his forever.

He moved slowly, wanting to make it last though he

knew his body wouldn't. Just looking at her—her eyelids heavy over those big brown eyes, her lips slightly parted and her body exposed and open for him—nearly pushed him to the edge. He bent down and kissed her, gently brushing the tip of her tongue with his as he began to stroke and thrust. Her gentle gasp caught his attention and he repeated the motion that caused it, sinking deeper and shortening his strokes so that the base of his shaft massaged her succulent folds.

The pressure built. He watched her breath go heavy and her eyes glaze. It was a beautiful sight, the pleasured glow of a woman near climax. He wanted to see it again and again.

"It's close," she warned with a roughness in her voice that was sexy as hell.

Propping her legs high over his arms, he dove in and pumped harder, thrusting and rocking, stroking her deep and hard until their bodies glistened and their breathing choked. And when her fervent cry pushed him over, he dropped her legs and pulled her close, clutching her in his arms as he lost himself inside her.

It seemed to go on forever, pulse after pulse strangling his throat and constricting his muscles until he finally collapsed in a sweaty, naked bliss. And with his face buried in the crook of her neck, he said in a muffled voice, "That was the best orgasm I've ever had."

She giggled. "I'll bet you say that to all the girls."

He pulled up and looked her square in the eye. "No. I don't."

Her playful expression sobered and she swallowed. "Well, you're pretty good at it yourself."

He could tell by the look on her face that he'd been more than pretty good. She felt what he felt only she was trying to keep the mood light. So he took her lead by hovering over her and casually raising a brow. "I have a few more fantasies, you know. You aren't in a hurry to get back to the party, are you?"

She smiled. "Party? What party?"

ALLIE BUTTONED HER BLOUSE while still giddy and glowing over the most amazing sexual encounter she'd ever experienced. Across the room, Nick was standing near the desk surveying the area with one hand on his hip.

"I seem to have lost my tie," he said.

She searched until she spotted a small swatch of green and red silk peeking out from one of the couch cushions. Snagging it, she held it up and twirled it in her hand. "This tie?"

His eyes met hers and they both grinned as they recalled how the tie ended up stuck in the couch.

"How could I forget?" He flashed her that sexy smoldering look of his that had a tendency to send off butterflies in her stomach.

She stepped to him and snaked the tie around his collar then went to work constructing a half Windsor. And as she did, a strange wave of familiarity washed over her. Clear as day, she could see herself in this same position decades from now, having tied thousands of ties for this man during the life they'd shared together. The eeriness of it gave her pause, but she quickly blinked and brushed it off. It was nothing but silly sentimental thinking—and dangerous given the circumstances, she told herself.

She'd propositioned Nick downstairs and ended up with a sexual tryst that had rivaled no other. But nowhere in this evening had either of them talked about intentions, futures and expectations. For all she knew, this was nothing but a one-night stand, and if it was, she had no right to be disappointed. That was what a woman got when she let lust take over before thinking things through.

But if you had your way...

The knot secured, she patted his chest, stepped back and walked across the room. Though she had no idea where this would go after they left this room, at the very least she wanted to clear the air so she could finally get rid of the year-long guilt she'd been harboring.

"Nick, about Halpin Technologies," she said. "I owe you an explanation and an apology."

"No, you don't, Allie."

"Yes, I do. Please." She wrapped her arms around her waist, suddenly uncomfortable for the first time since they'd kissed in the hall. She'd always kept her private life private, particularly at the office, but Nick deserved to hear this from her so he would stop apologizing for something that wasn't entirely his fault.

So she steeled herself and went on. "I moved to Chicago as a fresh start after spending three years in an abusive relationship." Noting the look on his face, she held up a hand. "It wasn't physically abusive, but emotionally it left scars. My ex was a narcissist who had somehow managed to take control of my life. He'd isolated me from my friends and family and somehow got me to believe I was incapable of surviving without him telling me what to do." She huffed, embarrassed to hear herself say the words. This wasn't something she talked about often, if ever. "You always believe it's the weak women who fall into those traps, but the truth is it can happen to anyone."

His voice was gentle and sympathetic. "I'm sorry."

She shook her head. "Don't be. I learned lessons and have come out a better person for it. But you have to understand that when I started here I was very headstrong and intent to prove myself capable."

Nick's shoulders sagged as realization kicked in. "And I waltzed in and bulldozed over you."

It wasn't how she would have put it, but she couldn't argue. "I wasn't open to criticism the way I might be if the same thing had happened today."

He placed a hand over his forehead and sighed. "God, I'm such an idiot."

"No." She crossed the room and stepped close. "Nick, you were right about Halpin. I really was doing it all wrong. If you'd left it alone, the whole thing would have blown up in my face."

"It wasn't my place."

"You were trying to help, but you'd hit a hot button with me and I grossly overreacted." She touched a hand to his cheek. "Please, stop blaming yourself."

He studied her for a long beat then cupped her face in his hands. And when he spoke, his voice was low and filled with regret. "I wasn't trying to help, Allie. I was trying to impress you." Remorse colored his expression as he took her hand in his. "When you walked in that first day, I thought you were the prettiest woman I'd ever seen. Then I got to know you and realized you were also smart as a whip. I was half-crazy in love with you within a week."

Her eyes widened.

"If you'd been anyone else," he went on, "I might have just asked you out, but you weren't. You were special. And before I made my move, I wanted you to think I was the greatest thing since video games." He shook his head. "I went overboard. And when you brushed me off, I went to Stryker not to rat you out or take the account away. I thought maybe if I couldn't convince you I was worthy, he could."

"Worthy. Worthy of what? A date?"

He raised her fingers to his mouth and kissed them.

"From that first day, Allie, I've wanted more than a date. I've wanted it all. You and me, the white picket fence, two-point-seven kids and a dog named Buddy."

Her jaw dropped.

"I'm crazy about you, Allie. I think I always have been. But in my eagerness I came on too strong and only pushed you away."

She stood there stunned, not entirely certain she'd heard everything correctly. Crazy about her? White picket fences? Her heart raced as reality sank in. So much for wanting more than just a one-night stand. Nick was offering her forever.

As she absorbed the situation, she admitted, "I wouldn't have been ready for this a year ago."

"What about now?"

A swirl of thoughts and emotions circled as the pieces of this past year snapped together. All her anger and animosity, the stabbing remarks and hurt feelings. It had started out as bitterness over what he'd done, but if she really allowed herself to acknowledge her true feelings, she knew somewhere along the line that anger became the end product of unrequited love.

Once she'd really gotten to know Nick Castle, she'd grown crazy for him, too. But by then the damage had been done. They'd entered a war that had no winners.

Until now.

A smile formed in her heart and spread across her face. "Now I think I could handle that just fine."

He slipped his arms around her and gave her a long deep kiss. "I won't screw this up again," he promised.

"You couldn't if you tried. We know each other a lot better now than we did then."

"But the one thing I've always felt is that you're the only woman who's right for me."

She pulled back and blinked. "Mr. Right. My Christmas wish to that weird Santa Claus was for me to find Mr. Right."

Nick laughed. "And I asked him for my dream girl."

"This is weird." The man's words came back to her. "He'd told me that if I looked inside my heart, I'd realize Mr. Right was there in front of me."

"And here I am."

She sank against his chest and rested her head on his shoulder, her heart warmed with the comfortable ease of their embrace. This embrace, this understanding between them and their confessions of the heart—it was like putting the square peg in the square hole and feeling the ease of the two sliding in place as they were meant to be. And it felt absolutely wonderful.

"And here I was trying to convince myself that Mr. Right could be Mike Holden." She stopped and gaped. "Mike! Oh, my, I left him down at the party."

Nick shrugged. "Something came up."

"But we should go down there. He could still be waiting."

"I'm in the mood for some champagne, anyway."

Hand in hand, they made their way back down to the party, and as she feared, the table was empty. Only the drink Mike must have fetched her sat there watered and warm.

"Uh, I don't think you need to worry about Mike," Nick said.

Allie followed Nick's gaze to a corner of the room where Mike was engaged in an intimate conversation with Jodi Hall.

Very intimate.

Allie wasn't sure if she should be relieved or offended. After all, she and Mike had been talking about getting together for dinner and a movie. Now, he was in the corner with Jodi, sharing sips of a drink and whispering seductively in her ear.

Then Allie remembered where *she'd* just been.

"I don't think I should interrupt. Do you?"

"Usually when a guy has his hands on a woman's ass, he'd like to be left alone." Nick took Allie's hand and led her to the dance floor, where the old fifties tune "You're All I Want for Christmas" played. "Besides, they're playing our song."

She grinned as he held her in his arms and began a slow sway. "We have a song."

Overhead, paper snowflakes sparkled in the light while real snow began to fall over Chicago. Out the windows, the twinkling skyline shone like candlelight for as far as the eye could see. And in her arms, Allie held the greatest gift of all.

"We have more than a song," Nick said. "We finally have each other."

You're All I Want for Christmas

1

ONLY SEVEN MORE SHOPPING days until Christmas. Staring at the pittance that was her check from the temp agency, it was obvious Anna Cole wouldn't be spending those shopping days at Saks or Neiman Marcus. Her final paycheck would barely cover the gas money to take her back home to Twin Falls, Idaho.

For good.

The thought put a damper on what, up until now, had been a pretty good day. An hour ago, she'd still been holding out hope that she'd find a way to stay in Chicago. She'd spent half her life pining to be here. Having to go back home stung deeply, but she had no choice. The job she'd been promised fell through, and what work she could find hadn't been enough to cover her college tuition and living expenses. After six months in the Windy City, she'd wound her options down to two choices: start living in her car, or stick her tail between her legs and go crawling back home.

She could already hear her family saying "I told you so." They'd all balked at her lofty goals to go off to college in the big city all by herself. Her mom had argued that there was a perfectly good school in Boise she could attend while living with Aunt Kate. Daddy didn't understand why she wanted to be a nurse when she'd just been promoted to cashier at Sam's Grocery Outlet. He'd told her union jobs were scarce these days and she should keep the good fortune she had. Besides, nobody went off to college at her age, he'd say, as though twenty-five was halfway to the grave.

Worst of all were her brothers Mark and Dean, who reminded her as often as possible that she was too stupid for medicine and that if she did manage to graduate from nursing school and get an actual job, she'd end up killing more people than she helped.

Okay, so Mark and Dean were only teasing like big brothers did, but that wouldn't lessen the pain when she had to walk back into the old sprawling ranch house and announce that she wouldn't be going back after Christmas break. For the most part, they'd all been right. She'd set off for the thrill of the big city and instead of offering her the exciting opportunities she'd sought, it only chewed her up and spit her out. And now, with only two semesters under her belt and her savings drained, she'd be heading back home without ever having done one single adventurous thing.

She sighed as she thought about all the things she'd wanted to do. She'd never made it to the ballet or the symphony. She'd never strolled down Michigan Avenue and gone into Tiffany's. Heck, here she was picking up her paycheck in the world-famous Willis Tower and she'd never even gone up to the Skydeck. She'd been too focused on settling into school, grabbing what work she could find and job hunting for more in all her spare time. She'd put the sightseeing aside for the day she was settled, but that day never came.

Forcing a smile on her face, she thanked the receptionist

and walked out of the agency, tucking the check into her purse as she made her way out. When she stepped into the elevator and hit the ground-floor button, she was struck with an impulse. Next week, she'd be on her way home. She had to do at least *one* fun thing while she was here. Even if she couldn't afford it, she really couldn't go back to Twin Falls without a solitary story to tell her friends and family. So on her way down, she decided to splurge on a going-away present and tour the Skydeck while she was here. She'd heard that even after dark the view was amazing at 103 stories up, and a tour of the Skydeck museum sounded way better than packing up to leave.

Maybe she'd even dare to step out onto the Ledge, those new all-glass enclosures that projected out from the building's edge and gave most people vertigo. Anna wasn't crazy about heights, but for the sake of saying she'd done something thrilling, she'd overcome the nausea and take a step out over the busy streets. As the elevator whipped down, she smiled, her happiness resumed temporarily as she contemplated an evening of fun.

The car came to a stop halfway down and she stepped aside expecting company. But when the doors opened, no one was there. She pushed the ground-floor button again and waited, but after too long nothing happened. The elevator just sat there with its doors open.

She pressed more buttons. Still nothing. Evidently, the thing was stuck. She stepped out and mused that at least it hadn't stranded her inside between floors. She'd wanted a thrill, but not that kind.

Shrugging it off, she pushed the button to hail another elevator and waited. Off in the distance she could hear Christmas music coming from a room down the hall and what sounded like a holiday party going on.

It took her back to her years at Sam's and the annual

holiday parties they always threw. Oh, that was always a fun night. The food was marvelous, the mood was bright. Couples danced and people gossiped about who was drinking too much or who was lusting over whom. They all dressed up, offering a rare sight of themselves in suits and dresses instead of Sam's red-and-black uniforms. As she waited for another elevator, she reflected with longing about those parties and that she'd missed it this year.

The familiar bursts of laughter from the room down the hall brought back memories. The thought of food made her stomach growl. She'd skipped lunch and it was past the dinner hour. Anxious to get home, she pressed the button again, but still nothing happened. The elevator she'd departed still sat there with its doors open and none of the others were coming to her rescue. So instead of waiting there indefinitely, she went off in search of the stairs, thinking maybe she'd have better luck on another floor.

Instinctively, she moved in the direction of the party toward a corridor she thought might lead to a stairway. And when she found herself in front of the noisy party room, the door suddenly flew open. An older man with olive skin stepped through and when he saw her, he held the door, apparently thinking she'd been on her way in. She began to speak, to excuse herself, when her eye caught the activity inside.

The room looked like a Christmas wonderland, with its lights turned low and decorative snowflakes hanging from the ceiling. Music played from the stage and crowds of people were mulling around, dancing, chatting and nibbling on food. Tables circled the perimeter of the room, which was informally decorated in green and red. But what really grabbed her attention was the mile-long buffet table packed with meats and salads and desserts.

Her mouth watered. She'd eaten little more than ramen

noodles and fast food for the past six months. And as she eyed the display, the absurd notion of stepping in for a bite crossed her mind.

Go in, the little voice said. *You're on an adventure, right? You wanted a story to tell your friends. Go in and have a bite. What's the worst that could happen?*

She blinked off the ludicrous thought of crashing some-one's party. Though as the man held the door for her expectantly, she noted he, at least, had no idea she didn't belong there. And judging from the number of people inside, she questioned whether anyone else would, either.

"You coming or going?" he asked.

She had to think fast. *Do it,* the little voice kept urging. *Step inside. If someone asks, just say you're lost. There could be a hundred holiday parties going on in this building tonight. So you showed up for the wrong one.*

"I, uh…" she stammered.

Are you on an adventure or not?

"Thank you," she said, quickly darting into the room while she had the nerve.

She shrugged out of her coat and moved toward the food where the largest crowd of people gathered. She'd intended to simply hang out for a moment and see how well she blended in, but as soon as she stepped near the tables a young man in Dockers and a green striped shirt casually turned to her and said, "The pork buns are going fast. Get them while you can."

"Pork buns?"

She watched as he shoved what looked like a buttery dinner roll in his mouth. Then he rolled his eyes in apparent bliss. "Alan Chan brought them from Chinatown. They don't make them like this in the burbs."

"Galen, your wife's chicken salad is wonderful," said

a woman to their left. She turned to Anna. "Have you tried it?"

"I, uh, just got here," Anna muttered.

Galen pointed a finger. "You're the new girl in Controller's right?"

She opened her mouth, not sure how to respond. She didn't have much practice crashing parties and lying through her teeth, but taking on someone else's identity didn't seem like the best idea.

"I'm just temping for a few days. They told me to stop in if I wanted."

There. That seemed as close to the truth as possible. And as her heart pounded she eyed the two and waited for signs of a problem.

The woman simply smiled and held out a hand. "I'm LaRhonda." She gestured to the plate in her hand. "Galen's in-laws own a deli. At every potluck function we insist he bring their famous chicken salad, but you better grab a plate. It won't last."

And just that easily, Anna was officially on her adventure.

"Another year, another trip to Maui." John Stryker Jr. patted the back of his friend, Nick Castle. "Congratulations on the top sales award."

Nick stepped away from the group of men he'd been chatting with. "Thanks, John."

"I don't know how you do it. Everyone had their money on Daryl this year after he hit it big with Jackson Pharmaceuticals."

"Not big enough, I guess."

"In my opinion, you deserved it anyway. You work harder."

"I do," Nick agreed. He took a sip of his drink and

added, "To me it's not work. When you love what you do it's like playtime."

John smiled and nodded despite the fact that Nick's comment struck a sore nerve. He'd give anything to know what it was like to love his job. Not that being second in command of Stryker & Associates exactly sucked. He'd been born into a gift plenty of people would kill for, and John would always be thankful for his fortune. But it seemed the more time he spent learning the ropes and priming his skills to someday inherit his father's company, the more he realized he didn't want it. Finance, numbers, risk management—insurance could be a risky business but not the kind of risk that got John's blood pumping. Despite his father's efforts to sell him on the business, John simply couldn't get excited about life behind a desk. And the closer he got to thirty, the more anxious he felt about the path he was on.

"Must be nice," he muttered.

Nick gaped. "Dude, it doesn't get *nicer* than being John Stryker Jr."

John eyed Nick then confessed, "White-collar work has never interested me."

"So what? You're rolling in dough."

John laughed, recalling the days when that very thought drove his plans for his future. As a young teen fueled by his father's urging to go into the family business, John hadn't argued. At the time, he'd only been thinking about the hefty salary, and for a kid only interested in fast cars and high-rise condos, taking over Stryker & Associates was a no-brainer. But it had been a while now since his interest in such luxuries had worn off, and being at the tail end of his youth he couldn't shake the idea that this career was a big mistake. He didn't share his father's interest in insurance, didn't have Nick's passion for sales, and as time kept ticking along his dissension had built.

"There's more to life than money," he said.

"Says the guy who's always had it." Nick pointed a finger. "Take it from the one who didn't. Money can buy a lot of happiness. Anyone who says otherwise didn't grow up on my street."

John smiled, knowing his friend was right. He did appreciate what he had, and if he was truly considering stepping down from his position, he knew he'd face more than the disappointment of his parents. Depending on what he ended up doing, he could be facing a serious lifestyle adjustment, too.

"All right. I suppose I can't argue with that."

He sipped his drink and watched the crowded room. So many people in this room had ambitious goals and dreams of success. Some of them had spent decades climbing the corporate ladder, but John was cutting straight to the top and wishing he were anywhere but here.

It didn't seem right. But at the same time, the thought of leaving this comfort zone wasn't exactly pleasant, either.

"So who are you taking to Maui this year?" he asked, feeling the need to change the subject. He had to remind himself that tonight wasn't the night to be stirring up doubts and worries. It was a time to celebrate a long year of hard work and give thanks to people who'd earned it.

Nick shrugged. "I've got no idea."

"What about the woman you're dating?"

"Pam? That ended ages ago."

John blinked. Had it been that long since he and Nick had shared a drink? "I'm sorry. I didn't know."

"Don't be. It was fun for a minute but there was nothing lasting there."

John opened his mouth to reply when a woman caught his eye.

No, not a woman, more like an angel.

She stood across the room near the buffet table, and was tapping her foot to the music and swaying her sexy hips the tiniest bit. She was beautiful, with curly brown hair, a petite turned-up nose and wide eyes filled with cheer. The prettiest thing he'd ever seen, though it wasn't just her looks that had him in rapture. It was the spirit she emitted, the bright expression on her face and a smile that seemed to light up the space around her. Just looking at her was like spotting a ray of sunshine cutting through the clouds, and as he stood and gaped, he was overcome with the urge to go strike up a conversation.

"What about you?" Nick asked.

"Me what?"

He wondered if she was married. Squinting, he tried to catch a glimpse of her ring finger from the distance but had no luck. The light was too dim and her left hand was wrapped around a fruity-looking drink that hid the view of her fingers.

"Maui, you and me and whatever island babes we meet along the way."

"Island…right." John gestured across the room. "Do you know her?"

Nick followed his gaze. "The woman in the pale blue blouse?"

"Yeah."

"Never seen her before. You?"

"No." But he intended to see her now.

He couldn't explain the instant pull. Over the years, he'd heard people talk about love at first sight and he'd always balked. Like anyone, he could appreciate an attractive woman from across a room, and he'd always assumed that was what they'd been talking about. Stretching simple admiration to actual love at first sight had always seemed pretty far-fetched. But now he had to wonder. The magnetism of this woman went beyond standard attraction, and while he certainly wasn't claiming love, he was no doubt consumed with the need to go talk to her. He wanted to hear her voice, to find out who she was and where she'd come from. He wanted to see the color of those sunny eyes and catch the scent of her hair. And judging by the itch in his jaw, he wasn't going to rest until he did.

As if she'd felt him staring she turned her head and met his gaze, and when she did, her sunny expression colored with interest. She'd already been smiling, but now the smile turned sultry, almost a little bashful, and sexy as hell.

Without switching her gaze from his, she took a sip of her drink. He could almost taste the sweetness on his lips, could practically feel those long slim fingers snaking down his chest. It was an odd sensation, one he'd never experienced before. And in the heat of it, he muttered a few absent words to Nick and set off across the room.

Love at first sight? Highly doubtful. But whatever it was, he intended to pursue it.

2

"ARE YOU ENJOYING THE PARTY?"

John's heart pounded as he struck up a conversation with the pretty brunette. He hadn't been this nervous around a woman since he was a teen, and as she looked up at him with those big brown eyes, he had to remind himself that he was a grown-up with experience and she was just another woman. Though it didn't feel that way. Instead, he felt giddy and awkward, and she felt special.

"I am. Thank you."

"I'm John." He extended a hand, anxious to touch her.

"I'm Anna," she said, putting a name to that beautiful face.

He liked it. The simplicity fit her. From this closer look, he could see that she wasn't made up or overly adorned. Aside from some frosty pink on her eyelids and a little gloss on her lips, she didn't wear much makeup, which was good. She didn't need to. With skin fresh as cream and a natural blush to her cheeks, anything more would just cover up her natural beauty. She wore simple posts on her ears, and around her neck was a heart-shaped locket he hoped didn't come from someone special. With a love life that had grown bland these past few years, he really didn't want to be shot down by the first woman in ages who actually stirred his blood.

"I don't recall seeing you around the office," he said. "Are you new?"

"I'm just a temp."

"Oh, for the busy year-end, no doubt. Who are you working with?"

Her high-beamed smile dimmed. "Oh, uh…" She fluttered her eyelids and stumbled. "I keep mixing up the woman's name. It's…"

He grinned and went for broke. "How about we forget that and I ask you the question that's *really* on my mind." He gently tugged at her bare wedding finger. "Are you spoken for, or am I free to ask you to dance?"

SOMEBODY PINCH ME.

Anna took in the gorgeous hunk and wondered if she was dreaming. She'd wanted a thrill tonight, and in her girl-from-a-small-town definition of thrills, that consisted of sneaking into a party to steal a yummy meal then climbing a hundred stories to catch a view of the Chicago skyline. Nowhere in that equation had been meeting a handsome businessman and sharing a Christmas dance.

And maybe more?

Judging by the smoldering look in his eyes, a dance might only be the first thing on his mind, and if that was the case, her night was getting more and more adventurous by the minute.

She held her grin back to a casual smile as she accepted his hand and said, "I'd love to dance." Then she followed him the few short steps to the dance floor right as the upbeat "Jingle Bell Rock" ended and the tempo slowed.

He made a face that said *how convenient* and moved close, slipping his hand around her waist. And when he nudged her toward him and settled his palm at the base of her spine a wash of tingles spilled over her skin.

Good gracious. When exactly was the last time she'd been touched by a man? It definitely hadn't been since she'd shown up in Chicago, and her on-again-off-again boyfriend back home had been on the off side for most of the year before that. It was safe to say that her sex life had been running cold for a long time, and if John was hitting on her tonight in the hope of getting lucky, he might very well have picked the right girl. She couldn't remember a time when such a simple touch packed this big a punch.

She quickly met his gaze, her head going a little dizzy over the sight of that strong jaw and his deep gray eyes. Those eyes had been the first thing she'd noticed when she'd spotted him across the room. They were dark and fiery, bold and compelling. And she'd caught them aimed straight at her. Immediately, she'd felt the heat in them smooth through her like a shot of stiff whiskey. And now the man himself was here in her arms, his chest brushing hers and their bodies held close as they swayed to the music.

This had to be what Cinderella felt like at the ball.

He bent in, giving her a whiff of aftershave that smelled subtle and expensive. "Tell me something about yourself, Anna," he said in a low, smoky voice.

She thought for a moment, wondering how she should respond. Being that this was her fantasy night, she almost wanted to make up something more exotic than her simple life. After all, she wasn't sure what John did for this company, but judging by the tailored suit and expensive-looking watch, he probably wasn't pushing the mail cart. He might be more enthralled by a more worldlier type of woman.

Unfortunately, she knew she'd never pull it off, so she opted for the truth. "I'm at UIC studying nursing."

Okay, so that was only true up to a week ago, but it was easier than explaining that at the moment, she wasn't really anything. She had no job and no money, and only a red Kia that would get her back home to Twin Falls. Other than that, her life was a blank slate. Not an avenue she really cared to go down tonight.

He smiled and her stomach did a flip. He was seriously handsome when he smiled. It brought out a set of faint dimples and made those dark eyes sizzle.

"Have you always wanted to be a nurse?"

Clutching her hand, he spun her in a circle and she giggled.

"Not exactly. I floundered a bit out of high school and only found my calling a couple years ago."

He eyed her quizzically. "How did that come about?"

She shrugged noncommittally. "Oh, just life."

In truth, it had been tragedy that both called her to nursing and taught her that life was short and precious, but she didn't want to go there, not tonight when the mood was so festive and her spirits so high.

"What about you? What do you do for—" *Crap, what was the name of this company?*

"I push paper," he offered. "Nothing nearly as interesting as medicine, and I must admit, I'm floundering a little myself these days."

He spun her around again and this time when he pulled her back in his arms, he moved closer. Now those firm thighs brushed against her hips and her nose nearly touched his jaw. Her stomach tingled—along with a couple other body parts—as she noted how close her lips would be to his if he only tilted his head just so.

"It's funny to hear you talk about finding a calling," he went on. "I've had one needling at me for a long time, but so far I've tried to ignore it. It sounds like we might have something in common."

As the smooth music continued to play they set conversation aside and focused on dancing. She liked the way their bodies meshed together, the long glide of his tall frame against hers. She noted how nicely her head might rest on his shoulders, how easily their lips would come together if their bodies were joined. The lustful thoughts got her body stirring, fueled by the sultry dance, and by the time the song finally ended, she was fully aroused.

"How about a drink?" he offered, either guessing or seeing on her face that she could use a cooler.

"That would be great."

They found a table near the windows and started chatting, and it wasn't long before Anna acknowledged her attraction to John was more than physical. She found him funny and easygoing, humble and charming. She told him about growing up in Twin Falls and the trials of having two older brothers. He shared the same woes about having two younger sisters. They talked about movies and music, hobbies and food. When the conversation wandered to his company, she diverted it away, fearful that any talk about work might blow her little white lie. Though the longer they talked, the more those little lies started piling into bigger ones.

He was so interested in her nursing studies that she kept talking as though her life wasn't on hold, and just like her mother had always warned, the lies bred like rabbits. Soon, her permanent trip back home became just a short visit for the holidays, and he was talking about introducing her to some people he knew in medicine when she came back after Christmas break. He wanted to make plans to see her in the New Year, and she couldn't dream up a good reason to say no. By the time their drinks were empty and he got up to fetch another round, she'd spun herself into so many tales that she was in dire need of a few minutes alone to think.

When this night started, she'd assumed this encounter with John was about one superficial fantasy evening. She wasn't supposed to adore him and he wasn't supposed to be interested in much more than getting in her pants. She'd flippantly tossed out tales assuming none of it would matter, but now he was talking about tomorrow and next week and she had no idea how to worm her way out.

Oh, Dean would be laughing right now telling her it was exactly what she deserved for sneaking into a party and making up stories. And in one of those rare moments, she'd have to agree with her brother. She'd talked herself into a web and now she had to get out. But how?

"I think I'm going to make a quick trip to the restroom," she said, rising from the table before John left for the bar.

"Go ahead. I'll grab a couple drinks and meet you back here."

She left the banquet room in search of the bathroom, all the while trying to come up with a way to come clean, but every scenario she conjured played out poorly. He didn't know that sneaking into parties and lying about her life weren't her regular pastimes. That normally, she was honest to a fault—literally. She could recant plenty of situations where a little white lie would have kept her out of trouble, but it had never been her nature. It was only tonight, with him, never before and never again.

Yeah, right. Surely he'd believe that.

Pushing her way through the bathroom door, she ran into LaRhonda, the woman she'd spoken to earlier at the buffet table. When LaRhonda caught her eye, the woman smiled and winked. "Well, look who it is. Are you having a good time?"

"Yes, it's a wonderful party," Anna replied.

"And lucky you, catching the eye of the company SOB. A dozen women are jealous of you tonight."

"The SOB?"

"John Stryker." LaRhonda moved to the sink and washed her hands while Anna stood and stared, not understanding the statement.

LaRhonda blinked. "Don't you know who he is? The SOB—Son of Boss. His father owns the company—and he will, too, someday."

Anna's stomach turned. "John owns the company?"

LaRhonda laughed. "Girl, you are a newbie, aren't you?" She shut off the water and grabbed a paper towel to dry her hands. "You know, half the single women in this company have hit on him and struck out. You're a lucky gal. He's a hot item around here." Moving to the door, she said over her shoulder, "You have fun tonight!"

And suddenly Anna was alone, confused, sick to her stomach and wishing on stars that she could start this night over again.

The owner's son?

Why hadn't she put that together? Though now that she knew, a couple of comments he'd made earlier now made total sense.

Oh, this was worse than she thought. Her lies had felt bad enough back when she thought he just worked for the company. The owner?

Her yummy meal began working its way north.

Her first instinct was to flee. She needed to leave this place, and fast, before she thoroughly humiliated herself. She had no business being here, and she definitely had no business toying around with someone as wealthy and powerful as John. What was a girl like her doing with a man like him anyway? Not that there was any future in it, because after all, she was leaving for good next week—not that he knew that, because according to him she'd be back in two weeks, but...

Oh, she was going to be sick.

For no real reason she turned on the faucet and washed her hands before leaving the bathroom, and when she got back to the table, John was waiting with a wide and innocent smile on his face.

Her throat tightened. "I'm sorry," she said when she stepped to his side. "When I was in the bathroom, I remembered I was supposed to be somewhere right now. I've got to go."

His smile turned to concern and he rose. "Do you need a ride somewhere? I've got a car in the garage."

"No, thank you, though. I'll be fine, but I'm sorry that I've got to cut our night short."

That big smile came back, but instead of leaving her giddy, this time it only pushed her near tears. "That's okay," he said. "We can continue this another time, right? I'd love to call you."

Short of words, she simply nodded and smiled.

He reached into his pocket and pulled out an expensive-looking pen and a.business card. "Here. Write down your number for me."

She stared at it and stumbled. "Oh, dear, um...how about you let me call you?" She accepted the card and read it. There it was. John Stryker Jr., Executive Vice President, Stryker & Associates.

How could she be so stupid?

"Are you okay? You look a little..."

He trailed off before adding the word *green,* but it was

exactly how she felt. She needed to get a grip before she really did humiliate herself.

"Yes, I'm fine. I'm just upset that I've got to leave. I was really having a wonderful time."

At least *that* was the truth.

She held up the card. "I will get back in touch after Christmas."

He seemed disappointed, but accepted her excuse. "Please do."

Then with a terse goodbye, she grabbed her coat and purse and jetted out of the room, no longer in the mood for a thrill or adventure. Instead, she was nauseous, hurt and angry with herself that she'd created such a mess. And as she hit the elevator button to take her out of this place, she swore to herself that she'd learned her lesson. No more making up stories or going places she didn't belong. And never again would she ever say anything that wasn't the God's honest truth.

3

JOHN WATCHED AS ANNA weaved through the crowd on her way out of the room, disappointed their evening ended before it had even gotten started. He'd wanted to spend more time with her, and not just because she was sexy and fun. There was something about her he found endearing and she'd sparked an energy in him he'd wanted to explore. On a night when he'd been searching for cosmic guidance, he'd almost felt as if he'd found it, only now she was gone, and he was back to the same nagging discontent that had consumed him an hour ago.

"You look like someone who could use some Christmas cheer."

John looked up to find a hefty man in a red silk suit standing at his side. The man was barrel-chested with rosy cheeks and a snow-white beard. He was balding, but the white hair he did have coiled almost to his shoulders, and when John looked him over, the first thought that came to mind was Santa Claus.

"You look like someone who can provide it," John said.

The man laughed with a very clichéd *ho-ho-ho,* then he gestured toward Anna, who was just pushing her way through the banquet doors. "That's the woman who can provide it."

"Yeah, well, unfortunately she had to go."

"And despite your strong feelings for her, you aren't going after her."

John furrowed his brow. "I offered to go with her. She turned me down," he explained, though why he was answering to this odd stranger, he didn't know. "Besides, we made plans to get together after the holidays."

"Ah, yes. You put your faith in the notion that she'll follow through."

"Are you suggesting she won't?"

"I'm thinking it's become your nature to step by and let opportunity pass. Going along is always easier, and you certainly can't say it's done you poorly."

John frowned and looked the man over. "I'm sorry, but do I know you? You seem to think you've figured me out, but I don't recall that we've ever met."

"I excel at my powers of observation, particularly the ones that tell me you're not satisfied with your life and where it's going."

John's eyes narrowed. "You've been talking to Nick Castle, haven't you?"

It made sense now, this weird man and his bizarre comments. John should have known better than to spill his guts to Nick, though it had never been Nick's M.O. to share confidences like that—especially to some oddball dressed up like a Vegas lounge version of Santa Claus. But it was the only explanation John could come up with.

"I listen with my eyes. I hear with my heart," the man said, apparently answering a question John hadn't asked. He took a small candy cane and placed it in John's hand. "You've been searching for answers and the woman who can provide them just walked out the door. In fact, all your life, answers have presented themselves to you yet you keep letting them flutter by. It's time you reached out and grabbed one before they stop coming along." The old man grinned and pointed a finger to John's chest. "But you know that, don't you? It's the reason for your discourse tonight. You're letting your life be decided by Fate, and while I'm a big believer in Fate, it only works magic when it's guided by free will."

"You lost me."

The man curled John's fingers around the small candy cane and held his fist tightly. "The answers won't come to you, young man. You have to go get them."

Then with a wink, he released his grasp and wandered off through the crowd.

For a long while, John stood and stared. That was pretty much the strangest thing that had ever happened to him. But despite it all, he couldn't shake the truth in the old man's words. The guy was right. Up to now, he'd been satisfied going with the flow, not making waves and doing what was expected of him. And it was making him miserable.

But he had no idea how Anna could change that. She could offer him answers? How was that possible when he barely knew the woman? Everything logical said it wasn't, but tonight wasn't exactly turning out to be a logical evening. He hadn't been able to explain his peculiar draw to her, either, or the sharp feeling of loss he'd felt as he'd watched her walk out the door.

The answers won't come to you, young man. You have to go get them.

It was a fortune-cookie anecdote that John should probably disregard. But as he tucked the candy cane in his pocket and set off toward the door, he figured what did he have to lose?

STUPID ELEVATORS.

What was wrong with this place? This was the Willis Tower, one of the most famous buildings in the world. It was a Chicago tourist attraction and home to some of the most prestigious businesses in America. You'd think they could have one damnable elevator that actually worked.

Anna pressed the button again as though it were attached to a buzzer that could wake someone up at the controls. She didn't need this delay. Every moment she stood there waiting, she had to fight off another urge to go back into that room and confess everything to John.

She'd liked him—had liked him a lot—and even though she was leaving next week and would never see him again, it still hurt to know that she'd lied and then taken off like she had. She felt awful, telling him she'd call when she knew she wouldn't. She'd been on the receiving end of that kind of thing before and it didn't feel good.

She pushed the button again and again before turning to go find the stairs. And when she did, she saw John coming down the hallway with a look of relief on his face.

"Good, you're still here," he said, stepping up to her side and placing a hand on her shoulder. His pleased expression only made her feel worse. "I know you said you had somewhere to go, but I wanted to see if you're free this weekend, maybe tomorrow. I really want to see you again before you leave."

She blinked, exasperated by that gorgeous hunk of a smile and the eagerness in his voice. So much so that when she opened her mouth to spout out some excuse, she found herself babbling out a total confession.

"Look, I don't work for your company. I'm not a student at UIC. I was, just not anymore. In fact, after the holiday, I won't even be coming back to Chicago." She wrenched her hands as she watched that eager smile slide from his face. "I shouldn't have taken your number and said I'd call. I just… Oh, this is horrible."

In a blathering gush of words, she spilled out her whole story from her plans to start an exciting life in a big city to the instant earlier in the evening when the elevator doors opened and stranded her on his doorstep. And as she talked, that pleasured look on his face turned.

"You aren't in nursing school?" he asked.

His expression was a mix of confusion and disappointment that tore at her insides and made her wish she could crawl into a hole.

"I was," she explained. "But I can't afford to stay. When I go home for the holidays, I'm going home for good. I'll have to pick up my studies somewhere near my family where I can utilize their help." She paused and gave him her best shot at poor puppy-dog eyes. "I'm really sorry. I should have been honest, but we were dancing and having such a nice time, I didn't want to ruin the mood with my sob story—not that I even belonged at your party in the first place." *Oh, how could this get any worse?* "It's just that I was so upset about having to leave Chicago, and when I came across the party, it looked like such a beautiful distraction. Everyone was having so much fun, and…"

She trailed off, having little more to say. There was no way to excuse her behavior and everything from this point on was just pathetic rambling.

His mouth cocked into a half smile. "You're telling me you're this upset over crashing our Christmas party?"

"It was dishonest."

The half-cocked smile widened. "And you only left because you thought I'd be angry?"

"I spent the evening talking myself into a corner and I didn't know how else to get out. Then I found out you practically own the place and I panicked. I'm so sorry. I can only imagine what you must think of me."

"I'll tell you what I think." He lifted his hand and touched a finger to her chin. "I think you're probably the sweetest person I've ever met."

She blinked, certain she hadn't heard that right. Or maybe he was playing with her. She definitely deserved it.

"I don't know how things are in Idaho," he went on. "But, sweetheart, crashing a party and telling a white lie about your career barely registers on the scale of misdeeds here in Chicago."

"You aren't mad," she observed.

"On the contrary, I think you're adorable."

A huge weight fell from her shoulders. "You don't know how awful I've felt. I thought it would be better if I left, but it only made me feel worse." She expelled a long breath. "I promise from now on I won't utter anything that isn't the honest truth."

A glint of something teasing crossed his eyes. "Really? Now, that's an interesting prospect." He rubbed his chin and smiled. "From now on, no matter what I ask, you'll tell me the truth?"

She eyed him warily not exactly sure what she was getting herself into. "That's right."

"We could have some fun with this," he muttered. "You said you were looking for an adventure tonight."

"Oh, I think I've had enough adventure for one—"

"Nonsense. One can never have enough adventure."

"I was just planning on visiting the Skydeck is all. I'm sure for someone who works in this building, that's not much entertainment."

"To tell you the truth, I've never been up there after dark. I wouldn't mind checking it out."

He took her hand and stroked his thumb over her fingers, and everything in her warmed. Was it possible that they could pick this night up from where they left off? She wanted it so badly she was almost afraid to hope.

"When are you leaving Chicago?" he asked.

"I promised the woman I'm renting a room from that I'd stay until Tuesday. She's out of town and I'm feeding her cat."

"Then I've got an entire weekend to show you the sights." She opened her mouth to argue but he stopped her. "And don't worry about money. It's my treat."

"Oh, I could never let you—"

He moved close and held a finger to her lips, trapping her words in her throat by his sheer proximity and that sexy silver-eyed smile. "Would you like to spend the weekend with me? And remember, you've promised no lies."

The teasing sizzle in his gaze made her gooey inside. Oh, the man was gorgeous—not to mention forgiving and kind. Why was a package like this still available? she wondered. With those chiseled features and sweet smiles, the way his tall slim frame filled his suit, and the charm that oozed from his pores, she didn't doubt he could take his pick of any woman in the building.

And this weekend, he wants you.

How was that for adventure? When was the last time a hot, wealthy man wanted to spend his weekend showing her around a big exciting city like Chicago? *Uh, never.* She was getting a second chance in a way that was ten times grander than she'd even imagined. For sure, she'd be a fool to pass this up.

In a giddy daze of lust and disbelief, she nodded. "Yes, I would."

He grinned and took her hand. "Then let's go have some fun."

4

"Wow, THIS IS NEAT. What a pretty view."

John leaned against the wall of the Ledge and waited for Anna to take a step onto the glass floor that projected out from the Willis Tower's exterior thirteen hundred feet over Wacker Drive.

"You're supposed to be looking at it from out here," he called to her.

Her brown eyes looked like bowling balls as she eyed the glass enclosure. As they'd made their trek up to the Skydeck and through the exhibits, she'd been all over the idea of fully experiencing the attraction of the world-famous building. That was until she'd stepped within three feet of the Ledge and stopped dead.

She'd been standing in the same spot ever since, white-faced and rooted to the ground despite his efforts to convince her it was safe.

"I can see fine from here. This is good. Way cool!"

He chuckled and mused that the woman was as beautiful bug-eyed and pasty-faced as she'd been downstairs under the sultry party lights. Which meant only one thing. He was crushing on her bad. Downstairs, he'd simply been attracted, intrigued by her looks and that special spark of something he hadn't been able to put a finger on. In the two hours since, he'd found himself falling hard.

She'd snagged his affections when she'd gotten so upset over lying to him about temping for his company. It was the type of thing most people wouldn't give a second thought, yet to Anna it was one notch shy of grand larceny. Why? Because by nature she was sweet and honest and caring, and what he'd seen of her since only confirmed those qualities.

He'd nearly had to beg her to let him cover the measly admission to the Skydeck. Letting him buy a couple of trinkets she'd picked up in the gift shop was out of the question. The woman wanted nothing from him but to spend time with him, which was a refreshing change of pace. He didn't get much of that, being John Stryker Jr., and it was just another etch on his heart for this woman.

"What are you going to tell those brothers of yours when you get back home?" he asked.

Her wide eyes darted to his.

"You can try to tell them you stepped out onto the glass, but they'll see right through you." He offered a sly smile. "Then you'll be hearing about it for years."

She pursed her lips. "How do you know so much?"

"I'm a brother."

As timid as a squirrel, she took two baby steps toward the big glass box and looked down. At their feet, miles of twinkling lit streets spread across the horizon like strings of white Christmas lights for as far as the eye could see. John figured it was probably a good thing that it was dark. One didn't quite get the perspective of how high they were as they would in the light of day. And noting the fright in Anna's eyes, she needed all the help she could get.

He stepped across the glass enclosure and offered his hand. "Come. I promise you it'll be okay."

She scanned the floor and eyed his hand as though she couldn't decide if it was a life preserver or a tool of death.

"I'm afraid of heights," she finally blurted.

"I sensed that."

"I don't know why I thought this would be fun. I guess I didn't know how much I feared heights until I got here. There aren't many skyscrapers in Twin Falls."

"Are there any?"

"Not a one."

"Look," he said, stepping closer and lowering his voice to a calm and soothing tone, "I know you want to do this."

The look in her eyes said he'd gotten that one right, though he hadn't needed the confirmation. He knew from the short time they'd spent together that Anna wasn't afraid of a challenge. It was another thing that had attracted him to her.

"Like I said before…you'll be kicking yourself all the way back to Idaho if you go back down that elevator without ever having stepped out onto the glass."

"It's a long way down."

"That's why it's so thrilling."

She bit her lip and nudged forward.

"Stop looking down," he said. "Look at me." He wrapped an arm around her shoulder and held her close. "We'll go together. Just one step onto the glass."

She slid her arm around his waist and held on tight, the needy press of her body bringing him all kinds of feelings of possession, protection and, most of all, arousal.

He swallowed hard.

"We'll only go right there," he said, pointing to a spot a mere two feet away. "Keep your eyes up and move with me. We're just looking out a window, that's all we're doing."

"It's just a window," she repeated.

"That's all it is."

Arm in arm, they slowly moved together onto the glass. She was as rigid as steel, her eyes were closed and her hand was grasped so tightly to his suit jacket she nearly tore it off his shoulders. But when he spoke softly and began smoothing his fingers over her shoulders he felt her relax.

"What do you think?" he whispered.

A tiny gasp escaped her lips when she opened her eyes. "It's beautiful."

She released her grip and touched her fingers to the glass, allowing him the opportunity to move behind her and wrap his arms around her waist. Instantly, she eased against him, cocooning into his arms like two familiar lovers might do while standing on a rooftop and staring at the stars. Naturally. Comfortably. Easy and right, as if they'd been partnered for a lifetime.

He rested his chin against her temple and soaked in a long luxurious breath, absorbing her sweet flowery scent and basking in the feel of her in his arms. A shiver ran through her and his cock twitched, the ache to get closer quickly building as they stood there over the city.

"I've never seen this view after dark," he said, feeling the need to distract his thoughts from the sexy woman in his arms and the quick flood of images of her naked and him buried deep inside that glorious core. He was getting hard and she was nestling more comfortably against him, a combination that would turn pretty embarrassing if they didn't make a break for it fairly soon.

"Christmas from the top of Chicago," she said. "It's amazing." She nudged a little farther out onto the glass platform. "It's like being in the movie *Titanic* when Jack and Rose are on the bow of the ship and the ocean is roaring underneath them."

"I'm king of the world!" he proclaimed, and she giggled.

"I love the way the lights sparkle off the snow. I'll bet this was beautiful just after the storm when everything was fresh," she mused.

"Or a sunset. I hear those can be stunning."

For the next half hour they stood and talked as the city buzzed with Friday-night life below their feet. John couldn't remember a time when he'd appreciated something as simple as staring at the city, but he liked it. For a while now, he'd been haunted with the feeling that part of his life was rushing by, that there was something important he needed to be doing, but he couldn't see what it was and didn't know how to find it.

Now he knew it was this. Warm company and simple pleasures. All the money in the world couldn't buy it.

You've been searching for answers and the woman who can provide them just walked out the door.

Those strange comments from that weird guy at the party came back to him, and he wondered if it was only the power of suggestion playing with him tonight. Surely, if someone was told that a cosmic force was at work tonight, even the most skeptical of minds would be checking over his shoulder wondering if it might really be there.

But then Anna turned and looked up at him, the bright smile on her face turning his heart into mush, and he knew that these feelings of serenity weren't all in his head. They were real, coming from the woman right here in his arms.

And he only had a weekend to figure out what to do with them.

5

ANNA GAZED OUT THE window of John's Lexus trying to figure out what she'd done to deserve such a wonderful evening. At every turn she kept expecting to open her eyes and find herself back in her apartment, this whole magical experience just a dream she'd somehow conjured up in her sleep. But it wasn't. She was really here in the flesh, sharing a wonderful night with this sweet and sexy man.

If she hadn't already been smitten by John Stryker, the gentle way he'd coaxed her out onto the Ledge had snagged her affections completely. She'd been terrified up there, not in any state to take a step onto that platform and actually look down. But when he'd spoken to her softly with exactly the right words then enveloped her in his strong, protective embrace, she felt as though there wasn't a thing on the planet that could harm her.

With a sigh, she nestled against the soft leather seat and eyed him as he steered the car through the city toward her house. If only she'd met him six months ago when she would have had more time to spend with him. It didn't seem fair to find such a treat of a man mere days before she had to leave. But just as quickly as that depressing thought entered her mind, she pushed it back out. If she'd learned anything from her experiences, it was never to waste today by pining over what might have been. Life was a gift, and right now that gift involved a romantic evening with an attractive, charming man. She wasn't going to let a second of it slip by unappreciated.

"It's that house with the big tree out front," she said, pointing to the three-story brownstone where she lived.

He pulled up to the curb and shut off the engine.

"No one's home," she said. "Why don't you come in? I'll treat you to a cup of coffee—or something."

She slid him a sideways glance, hoping to make clear exactly what that "something" was.

His pleased expression said he got it loud and clear. "I'd love…something."

She led him up to the second-story apartment where she rented a room from an older woman who had been widowed several years back. While it lasted, the arrangement had been ideal. Irene O'Connor lived a quiet life, which helped Anna when it came to her studies. With both of Irene's grown daughters now living out of state, the woman rented the room more for the company than the money—which meant rent had been cheap. She and Anna had gotten along well, both having some vacant space in their lives that they'd filled with each other. And no matter where Anna ended up a year from now, she would always keep in touch with her new friend.

But at the moment, Irene was in Kentucky enjoying an early Christmas with her oldest, which left Anna delightfully alone to entertain a sexy businessman with an evening of…something.

"Have a seat," she said as she pulled off her coat and tossed it on a nearby chair. "I'll see what we've got to drink."

"Sounds great." He shrugged out of his wool coat and

suit jacket and set them over hers, then stepped into the front living room as Anna went to raid the fridge.

When she came back a few minutes later with a bottle of wine and two glasses, she found John near the Christmas tree toying with the knitted snow hats Anna had been making as gifts for her brothers.

"Whose are these?" he asked.

"Mine. I'm afraid that's all my family's getting this year, and that's only thanks to a big sale at the craft store."

She set the wine down and took one of the hats in her hand. "These are for my brothers. I've made scarves for my mom and dad."

"Wow, you're good. Do you know what they charge for these at the specialty shops?"

She shook her head, feeling more pride than she should over the simple compliment.

He pulled the hat down on his head and she laughed. The green-and-yellow knit cap with the fluffy pom-pom on top, ear flaps and braided tassels made an odd fashion statement when combined with John's white dress shirt and red holiday tie.

"How do I look?"

"Like a snowboarder on his way to court." She moved close and gave him a sultry smile. "Maybe if you lost the formality." Placing her hands on his chest, she began loosening his tie.

He raised a brow in intrigue. "Yeah, maybe the tie," he said, the humor in his voice sobering to something seductive.

His gaze moved to her lips as she slowly unraveled the knot, tug by tiny tug. Desire began to fill the air, weighing heavy and still like a fog forming over the room. It pooled low in her belly and warmed her skin, and as her fingers worked, she had to stifle the urge to go up on tiptoes and take a taste of that strong square jaw. Instead, she slipped the tie from his collar and tossed it on the table next to her knitting basket.

She quirked a brow and shook her head. "It's still not quite right."

"No?"

The molten look in his eyes said he was only playing along, anxious to see where she intended to take this seduction and being ready and willing to go wherever that was.

She went to work on his shirt buttons, tugging open the top one before biting her lip and moving to the next. His heavy breath caressed her fingertips as she spread the fabric to reveal the first hints of the smooth muscled chest underneath. Her mouth watered for a taste of it, and her body tingled with the thought of that warm breath wafting over her naked breasts. By the time she got to the third button, she'd gone from warm to hot to aching for some serious action.

She cleared her throat. "I think the problem is this whole shirt just needs to go."

"I think you're right." In one slow move, he pulled the hat from his head, slipped his arm around her waist and closed his mouth over hers.

A luxurious wave of liquid heat poured through her at the taste of those lips and the feel of his firm arms holding her close. It smoothed over her like a bubbly warm bath, swiping the tension from her shoulders and draining the strength from her limbs.

With a sigh she leaned into the embrace. She'd wanted this all night—had wanted more—and now that she had it, she wasn't disappointed. The man felt like pure bliss, and what he did to her body and senses was nothing short of splendor.

She coiled her arms around his hips and cupped his ass, smoothing her body close as a rapidly growing erection filled the space between them. It was long and impressive, the thick ridge surging sensation where it circled low and began to thrum into a slow, steady pulse. The scent of sex and man hung thick. And when he dug his fingers into her hips and squeezed, that slow pulse picked up speed.

"You're amazing," he whispered through the kiss. "I've been half-crazed for this since I first held you on the dance floor."

He moved his kisses from her lips to her chin then started a path down her throat. Tilting her head back, she closed her eyes and moaned. "This would be so much better naked."

"This would be more than a kiss if we were naked."

"I want more than a kiss." She trailed a finger over his thick ridge, just to make sure he didn't misunderstand. "Lots more."

It was all the prompting he needed.

Letting out a low growl, he scooped her into his arms and carried her across the room. "Sweetheart, you don't have to tell me twice."

He deposited her on the first soft place he could find, which was the large sectional sofa only three feet away, then moved to take her in his arms, but she pushed him back and straddled his lap instead. She couldn't remember ever wanting a man so badly, and now that she had him, she intended to take full advantage.

Tossing off her shirt and bra, she exposed herself to him, relishing the feel of his warm palms as he placed them on her breasts.

"These are beautiful," he groaned.

He nibbled at her skin before taking her breast in his mouth, smooth pleasure snaking down her spine and leaving her aching for more. His tongue felt like spun satin, he smelled like fresh soap, and as he licked and sucked, she lolled her heat to the side and let the sensations consume her.

"Oh, that's good," she uttered in a husky voice. His expression had grown dark and fiery, filled with a hunger that surged her pulse and heated her flesh. If the man had been sexy before, he was deadly now with that hot needy look in his eyes. It revealed strength she hadn't seen before, a focused intent that went beyond simple lust.

She tugged the shirt from his slacks and shrugged him out of it, revealing a body deliciously sculpted. It wasn't at all what she'd expect of a man who'd proclaimed to "push paper," and as she ran her hands over his firm, smooth skin, her curiosity grew. Who was this man who could be so gentle and friendly one moment then hot and sultry the next? What made him laugh? What made him burn? Oh, she wished she had the time to unravel all his secrets. Instead, she'd have to settle for the few she could uncover this weekend—most notably how this strong sexy body would feel inside hers.

Clasping her waist, he pulled her up from his lap so that her navel was at his lips. "I need a taste," he said, using quick fingers to unzip her pants and slip them down below her thighs. Then he bent low and opened his mouth over her mound.

Glorious sensations coiled through her and she cried out with a sound that was half gasp, half moan. She couldn't remember the last time she'd felt this luxurious, and as he began to stroke and lick, she shrugged off her pants to give him better access.

His throaty groan seduced her, weakening her knees and pushing her body toward an edge she didn't want to reach too soon. She wanted the night to last, had more things she wanted to explore, so just as she neared the peak, she slipped off the couch and knelt between his legs.

"It's my turn." She reached for his zipper and watched his expression sizzle. His lips were moist, his strong jaw flushed, and as she coaxed him out of his slacks, awareness deepened his already smoldering gaze.

His stiff cock sprang up between them and her clit pulsed in response. She wanted to feel the fullness in her womb, but the man was making her crazy. Before this went any further, she wanted him crazy, too.

She closed her mouth over the tip and sucked him in. His shaft jerked and swelled, and as she began stroking the smooth length, a guttural moan oozed from his lips.

"You'll be the death of me," he muttered with a sexy growl, but instead of attempting to pull away, he laced his hands through her hair and coaxed her along.

Lightly, she toyed, using her tongue to moisten his hard cock then blowing cool air to calm the force. Over and over she worked him, hot then cold, hard then soft, letting his low moans sing like music until his breath shuddered and he quickly jerked away.

"My pants," he said, his voice tight with need. "I've got a condom."

She retrieved it and sheathed him, then climbed on his lap and hovered over his tip. She ached to slide down over him but she forced herself to go slowly, wanting to draw out these pleasurable moments for as long as she could. With a sly smile, she teased herself over him, sliding down onto the tip then backing off, going a little farther next time then pulling away. His hands fisted at his side and his jaw clenched tightly, his need to take her quickly obvious in his eyes. But like her, he held back, letting the sensations percolate slowly.

He cupped her face in his hands, drew her lips to his and

kissed her, tangling his tongue with hers while she slowly and torturously eased him into her tight space, the thick length filling her and snatching her breath. And when she'd finally settled fully, she paused, wanting to simply relish the connection of their bodies fully joined.

Her heart pounding in her chest, she bent close and whispered, "I love the way you fill me."

"It's pretty good from this end, too."

Holding her hips, he gently began rocking, slowly at first then building momentum as they found a smooth rhythm. The room was cool but their bodies were hot, and soon a moist sheen covered them both as they neared the edge.

He reached between them and began stroking her clit with his thumbs, the sharp surge of pleasure quickly pushing her back to that edge. And as he circled and stroked, her body began to tremble.

"Go, baby," he urged. "Come for me."

He didn't have to ask twice. Just the urgent look of restraint on his face pushed her over, and as she held his shoulders and came, he groaned out a breath and came with her.

It was a tidal wave of pleasure that seemed to go on forever, their bodies bucking and thrusting until there was nothing left but the faint rippling of sensation that echoed and pulsed. And when her body finally calmed, she laid her head on his shoulder and sighed. "That was really, really good."

He turned his head and pressed a kiss to her cheek.

"Promise me we'll do that again before the weekend is over," she added, though the thought of this weekend ever being over sliced through the moment.

She brushed it off as he closed his arms around her and agreed, "Oh, yeah. We'll definitely be doing that again."

6

JOHN POURED TWO GLASSES of the wine he and Anna hadn't gotten to the night before. The moment they'd shed their clothes, things like food and drink were shoved aside for another time. As was sleep.

But now, after spending half the evening making love and an entire day touring the sights of Chicago, they were thankful to relax on Anna's couch with their containers of take-out Chinese food and her bottle of Two Buck Chuck.

He'd offered to get dressed up and take her out to an upscale restaurant for dinner, but she'd shot him down, arguing that he'd already spent enough money on her and that Irene's cat, Korky, got grumpy when left alone all day. So they'd settled for a casual meal in the living room next to the Christmas tree and a roaring fire, and John couldn't have been more pleased. He got enough fine dining on the job. What was really lacking in his life were these relaxing times in a comfortable place with a beautiful woman and good food. Heck, even the cheap wine tasted like ambrosia as long as he was sharing it with Anna.

Handing her a glass, he held up his in a toast. "To a wonderful weekend with a beautiful woman."

Her smile lit the room. "It's been more than wonderful. It's a fantasy Cinderella weekend I'll never forget."

She tapped her glass to his and took a sip, unaware that her words bothered him. He hated that she was leaving Monday. Every hour spent with her left him hungry for more, and the idea that this would be over in two days didn't sit well at all. Only he had no idea what to do about it.

In a heartbeat, he'd give her whatever money she needed to stay, but he knew she'd never accept it. And really, he couldn't argue with her objections. Despite how he felt, they still barely knew each other, and borrowing money from him was no way to start a budding relationship. But damned if he could stomach the thought of simply letting her walk away. So after much contemplation, he'd decided his only option was to find out as much as he could about her and hope that a solution somehow revealed itself before their time was over.

"So tell me about your nursing career," he said. "You said you'd discovered a calling. How did that happen?"

Some of the fun in her expression sobered. "It's not a pleasant story, really."

Recognizing the sudden sadness in her eyes, he placed his hand over hers. "I'm sorry. You don't have to talk about it if it upsets you."

She shook her head. "No, I don't mind. It's sad but it was a pivotal point in my life that changed everything about me. It's important."

She took a sip of her wine and began to tell him about Kelsey, her best friend since childhood who was killed in an automobile accident two years earlier.

"We were on our way home from Jackpot," she said. "We'd just spent the weekend at the casino and were having a great time, laughing and gabbing and daydreaming about all the places we wanted to see someday. Then out of the blue, we came around a bend and an eighteen-wheeler was in our lane."

"You were in the car with her?"

She nodded. Placing her hand on the fat calico cat sitting next to her, she began to pet his soft fur as she went on. "I don't know how I escaped without a scratch, but Kelsey was hurt bad. She was bleeding and crying. I found my cell phone and called for an ambulance, and it took what seemed like hours for one to show up. I was with her in the car, rode with her in the ambulance and watched her fade away before they had a chance to even get her into surgery." She winced. "I was the one who told her family that we'd lost her."

John stilled. "Oh, babe, I'm sorry." He cupped her hand in his, touched by the strength he saw in her eyes as she retold the story.

"It was a tough time, but it changed me forever. Before the accident, I was going along without thinking much about my future. My job didn't challenge me, and though I'd always wanted to someday experience life outside of Twin Falls, I'd always thought I had the rest of my life to get there. Now I'm not wasting time. I'm following my dreams and appreciating every day I have on this earth."

"And your dream was becoming a nurse."

She shook her head. "Actually, no. Before the accident, I didn't really know what I wanted. The only things I dreamed about were someday hitting Disneyland or maybe meeting Brad Pitt." Shrugging apologetically, she added, "I was pretty much your average ambitionless twentysomething, content to take whatever came along."

The comment hit close to home. Though John had excused his choices based on who he was, he couldn't deny that taking the job at his father's company was any different. For him, that was the easy route, the one that didn't make waves and basically landed in his lap. But despite the prestige and pay, he knew it wasn't the life he wanted.

"Nursing was a skill I uncovered after the crash," she explained. She closed her eyes for a moment and lowered her voice. "It was a really bad scene. Kelsey was in pain and sometimes hysterical, and as her injuries began taking the life from her..." She paused to swallow the emotion in her throat. "That was very difficult."

"I'm sorry," he said, squeezing her slim hand in his.

"Through it all, I stayed calm and in control, and afterward, the EMTs told me I was a natural. I spent some time with the hospital pastor, who got me to understand how important I was to Kelsey in her final hours. That as humans we can't control who lives or dies, but the support and comfort we give each other in those final hours makes a difference."

With a deep breath she picked up her wineglass and took a sip. "In the months after, I realized I wanted to become a nurse. It was something I knew I'd be good at, and it was a career that would give me purpose. I want to be there for people when they need help, and go home each day knowing that I'd done something that made a difference in someone's life, no matter how small a gesture it might be."

"It's an honorable profession that requires a special kind of person," John said. And he didn't doubt Anna was that kind of person. He'd already seen her unique mix of strength and compassion, and he could easily see that combination translating well into the field of nursing. He sure wouldn't mind having her at his bedside if he were ever hospitalized.

Drawing her close, he cupped her chin in his hand and

pressed a gentle kiss to her lips. "I'm only sorry you had to go through such a horrible experience in order to find that out."

The pretty smile returned to her face. "It was horrible, but I know Kelsey wouldn't have wanted it to destroy me. I think she'd be happy knowing something good came of her death. That's very important to me. Without it, her loss is just a tragedy."

For a few minutes, he sat and studied her, admiration and respect welling for this amazing woman who kept sinking further into his heart. He wondered how he would have fared if life had tested him like that, and he knew it was a question that might never be answered unless he stood up and took a chance.

"I've always wanted to be a cop," he found himself blurting.

She reacted with surprise, which was pretty much the same response he'd gotten from the few friends he'd confided in.

"What made you choose your father's company instead?"

He grinned. "That same ambitionless twentysomething mentality."

She picked up her container of chow mien and started digging through the noodles with her chopsticks. "I'd hardly call running a big company like that ambitionless."

"Not in the typical sense, but it was the path of least resistance. The job was handed to me. It's what my folks wanted, and it was hard to turn my back on the money."

She took a bite of her food and studied him while chewing, finally saying, "But you'd always wanted to be a cop."

"Ever since I was old enough to know what they were."

"So are you thinking about changing careers?"

"Quite a bit lately."

"What's stopping you?"

He chuckled. "You're the first person to ask me that. When I've mentioned it to friends, they mostly scoff at the idea and laugh like I've lost my mind."

"Why? What's wrong with being a cop?"

"I'd be walking away from a very hefty salary at a company where I'd ultimately rule the roost."

"But do you want to rule a roost?"

"It doesn't excite me, no."

Shrugging, she casually went back to her meal. "Well, you know what I think of that. We only get one turn in life, so you better make it good."

She made it sound so simple, as if giving up wealth and power for a job where he would be underpaid and underappreciated—not to mention the potential dangers—was a no-brainer. But maybe it was. Maybe his problem was that he spent too much time overanalyzing his choices and worrying about everyone but himself.

Then again, maybe it was only simple to Anna because she didn't realize exactly what he'd be giving up. She hadn't really experienced his lifestyle, didn't see all the perks that came with a high-powered career. She might not understand that he was talking about things bigger than a job switch.

"I make a lot of money," he said.

She eyed him over her box of chow mien. "Is that important to you?"

He blinked. Funny, how he'd been spending months asking himself that very question, wondering where his priorities should be, what he really wanted out of life. Yet when she phrased the question like that, it seemed to boil down to that one simple concept.

"It used to be," he said honestly. "Not so much anymore."

Especially not since he started spending time with Anna. These past twenty-four hours had brought him more joy and peace than he'd felt in a long time. They'd spent the day bombing around Chicago, visiting attractions he hadn't seen since he was a kid and enjoying the simple pleasure of interesting company and a casual meal. It had been joyful and relaxing.

In contrast, he knew his father's life. The job was much about sales and appearances. And it wasn't a job that ended Friday night. It was round-the-clock, lots of travel, speaking engagements, lobbying, wining and dining. His dad caught moments with his family, had been there on all the most important occasions, but one eye was always on the job. He had a phone planted to his ear and a BlackBerry glued to his hand. So for a long time now, John had been wondering if that was really the future he wanted. And for a long time now, he'd struggled to find the answer.

The weird Santa Claus from the party popped back in his head, giving him an eerie feeling.

You've been searching for answers and the woman who can provide them just walked out the door.

John wasn't supposed to believe in the unbelievable, but that brief conversation had been tugging at the back of his mind all day. And as crazy as it sounded, the more time he spent with Anna, the more credence he gave to the man's words. Something cosmic *was* going on here, and even though his head screamed that it was all a bunch of malarkey that had to be dismissed, his gut urged him to take a chance on faith. And when he did—when he really dug deep and tried to listen to his soul—he knew that the life of a businessman wasn't what he wanted.

"I've been thinking seriously about leaving the firm and

pursuing a career in law enforcement," he said. "But it's not going to be easy."

"I can imagine."

"My mother comes from a long line of cops. She always said the best move she made was marrying a civilian. She wouldn't be happy. My dad is expecting to leave his company in my hands someday. Each and every one of my friends will think I've lost my mind."

Quirking her brow, she set their containers on the coffee table and slipped onto his lap, wrapping her arms around his neck and leveling those sinful brown eyes with his. "Sounds to me like you've spent a lot of time worrying about everyone but yourself," she said.

His lips curved into a smile. "That's about right."

"What do *you* want?"

Sitting there on the couch with the sexy woman on his lap, he knew exactly what he wanted. Yes, it was to find a career he was passionate about, and when he boiled it down, he knew Stryker & Associates wasn't it. He wanted a new life that was wholly his, but he also wanted this woman in it.

Cupping her face, he drew his mouth to hers and absorbed all that strength and wisdom in one long, luxurious kiss. Where before he'd always doubted his choices, this time he could see what he wanted with absolute clarity, and it wasn't a fancy car and a high-rise condo. It was a deep soul-melding love with a woman like Anna who could light his fire and keep him real. It was life in a simple brownstone in a neighborhood where he was a real part of the community, doing a job that got his blood pumping and then coming home every day to a woman who would calm it down and smooth it over.

"I want this," he whispered, sliding his hands around

her waist and snagging another taste of what that life could be like if he could only keep her here.

And before Monday, he was determined to find a way to make that happen.

7

ANNA PACKED UP THE last of her things, going over the house once more to make sure she didn't leave anything behind. Tomorrow morning she'd be hitting the road early and she wanted to be organized and ready before enjoying her final evening here with Irene.

"You'll be back," the woman said as she stood in the hallway, answering to what must be obvious sadness on Anna's face. "Once you get your nursing degree there will be lots of good-paying jobs waiting for you here. It will be easier without the pressure of paying for school on top of everything else."

Anna smiled, appreciating Irene's words of support. And she knew it was true. Once Anna figured out she'd bitten off more than she could chew, she hadn't abandoned her idea of living in Chicago forever. She'd simply accepted the fact that while she carried the burden of paying for school, she would need to stick closer to home, where her family could help with living expenses. She'd already discussed with Irene the idea that once she had her credentials, she could come back and give the city another try.

It had felt like a good consolation prize at the time. She

wasn't giving up her dreams she'd simply had to make an adjustment.

But that was before she'd met John.

Last week, she'd simply been disappointed at having to put life in Chicago on hold for a couple more years. Now she was leaving both the city and Mr. Wonderful behind, which took her disappointment and turned it into anguish.

She took a seat on the couch and let out a long breath. "I really liked him, Irene."

She hated the whiny sound in her voice. It went against everything she was supposed to live by. This last weekend had been wonderful. Thanks to John, she'd seen more of the city than she'd ever imagined, had spent her last three days on an enchanted adventure of sightseeing and romance. She was supposed to be thankful for the gift she'd been given, but no matter how much she told herself that, her heart wouldn't listen. Truth was she'd really liked him. She'd liked him a *lot*. And having to leave right at the point where something might have come from their relationship colossally and royally sucked.

Even telling herself that things might have fizzled between them over time didn't help. After only two days together, it was hard to guarantee that they would make it for the long haul. But thanks to her situation, she'd never know. She was going back home and leaving unfinished business behind, destined to spend the rest of her life forever wondering if this man might have been the love of her life. He'd sure as heck felt that way.

Never in her years and relationships had she ever connected with someone so deeply and quickly as she had with John. And though she kept reminding herself that they hadn't been together long enough for her to draw those kinds of conclusions, she couldn't shake the feeling in her heart that she was leaving someone really amazing.

"He sure sounds like a winner from what you told me," Irene agreed. The woman sat down on the couch next to Anna and placed an arm around her shoulder. "But if it's meant to be, you two will find your way back to each other."

Anna nodded, knowing it was true. She told herself that life had a course that we could only partially control. The rest we had to give up to Fate. She knew that, and had accepted it for the most part ever since Kelsey's death. But right now it didn't make her feel better. Right now, she really hated Fate and all the crappy things it had taken from her life.

She released a long breath and sighed. "I'm in a bad mood and I need to snap out of it," she admitted. Moping wasn't going to change her situation. It was only going to make her feel worse and she didn't have room in her life for self-inflicted pain.

"What do you say we go down to the corner and get burgers and milk shakes at Rosie's Diner?" Irene suggested.

Anna smiled. "For my last meal in Chicago? I can't think of anything better." She patted Irene's thigh and rose from the couch. "You can tell me all about Kentucky while we're there."

The two women grabbed their coats and headed down the stairs, Anna feeling better having finally made the decision to shape up and move on. Yet when she opened the door, she found John standing there, his finger pointed as though he were just about to press the buzzer.

All the hurt and sadness she'd just shrugged off came back twofold. Oh, the man was handsome in his sharp suit and dark wooly overcoat. And as she watched him standing there grinning, those faint dimples pressed in his cheeks and his silver eyes bright with affection, the loss fell on her shoulders like actual weights.

"John. I didn't expect you until later."

Apparently oblivious to the sadness in her eyes, he reached out and pressed a cheery kiss to her lips. She swallowed back the lump in her throat. How could he be so pleasant and upbeat and not feel the slightest disappointment that these sensual kisses would soon be a thing of the past? Apparently, her feelings for him had amounted to more than his feelings for her, and the reality of it made her feel silly. Growing attached to the man in two measly days. What was she thinking?

He backed up a step and held out his hand to Irene. "You must be Irene. Anna told me good things about you."

Irene lit up like the tree in her living room. "And she wasn't kidding when she told me you were handsome and charming."

Anna blushed as John chuckled.

"We're on our way to Rosie's for a late lunch," Anna said. "Would you like to join us?"

He shook his head. "No, I'm sorry but you'll have to change your plans. You've got a job interview."

She blinked. "A what?"

"It took me a while, but I found a guy down at the Mason Street Clinic who has an opening for a nurse's aide. I told him all about you and he wants to meet you this afternoon."

Her jaw bobbed as her eyes darted to John then Irene then back to John. "But, John, I can't—"

"You need a job, isn't that right? That's why you're leaving."

"Yes, but—"

"Okay, so the pay probably isn't the greatest, but it's more than minimum wage. And here's the best part. Once you've been there six months, you're eligible for his educational assistance program." His giddy grin widened. "He'll pay for your schooling, but only for as long as you're working there and only after you've passed the probation period."

She stepped back, all this information too much to absorb so quickly. A job that would pay for her schooling? "I don't know if I'm qualified."

"You said you'd been volunteering at the hospital back in Idaho."

"Yes, before I left, but—"

"It's all he needs."

She stood gaping at him and stunned, trying to believe what she was hearing. It sounded wonderful. It sounded better than wonderful. It was a dream come true. But her problems had gone beyond simply needing a job.

"John, I really appreciate it, but I can't even cover next month's rent. This would have been great if I'd gotten it a month ago, but now—"

"Forget about rent," Irene said. "You can start paying me again after you start getting regular paychecks. Consider it a Christmas gift."

Anna turned to Irene. "I couldn't let you—"

"You don't have a choice, hon." Irene slid a glance toward John then turned back to Anna with that stern look in her eyes that said she was serious. "This is a great opportunity. You can't let it slip away. Besides, I don't have a new tenant lined up. I was going to have to lose a couple months' rent looking for someone anyway. I'll gladly let it slide to keep you here."

"I—" She didn't know what to say. "I'll pay you back. I'm sure my parents will give me money for Christmas. They always do. It won't be a lot but it'll be a start—"

Irene looked at John. "Does she have trouble hearing?"

John laughed. "I think your problems are solved." He coiled an arm around Anna's shoulder and pulled her close. "Babe, I've spent all morning on the phone finding a way to keep you here. I called in favors and pulled all kinds of strings. You can't let me down now."

"Let *you* down?"

"Yes, because if you don't stay, I'll be forced to follow you to Twin Falls." He held up a hand. "Don't take it wrong, I'm sure it's a nice place to live, but I'd rather not have to leave Chicago chasing after the woman I'm crazy about."

Irene clapped her hands together. "I'm going to go drag out the champagne. I've been saving for a special occasion just like this." She quickly turned and headed back into the house.

Anna's heart swelled. "You'd follow me to Twin Falls?"

He cupped her face in his big warm hands. "Anna, I don't know about you, but I feel something special between us, so special that I can't let you walk out of my life before we pursue it and see where it goes."

She let out a sigh of relief. "I feel that way, too."

"Then you'll stay and check this job out? Let your friends help you?"

"I'd be crazy not to."

He pulled her into his arms and treated her to a long glorious kiss. It felt so good she thought she was dreaming. It was almost too much to take in, the thought that she wouldn't have to leave her lofty goals behind, that she could stay and enjoy these heavenly kisses and the sweet, sexy man offering them.

A shiver of excitement ran through her, making her giggle. "I can't believe this. I can't believe you've done this for me."

"Don't give me that much credit. It's selfish, really. I want you nearby. Over the next few months, I'm going to need all the support I can get." Squeezing her hands in his, he added, "After the New Year, I'm leaving Stryker and joining the police academy."

She gaped. "You're going to do it?"

"You've given me the inspiration I needed to take the plunge."

"Are you sure? It sounds like such a big move."

"It is, as soon as I'd made the decision I knew it was right. I'm happier than I've ever been."

"I think that's wonderful!"

"Yep." He hugged her tightly. "That weird old guy back at the party was right. I was searching for answers and he said I'd find them with you."

She eyed him quizzically. "What weird old guy?"

"I think it was Santa Claus, though I can't be sure."

"And he said you'd find answers with me. That sounds... unbelievable."

He laughed. "I think the word is *kismet*."

"Kismet." She rested her head on his shoulder and reflected on the weekend, from the moment that elevator mysteriously dumped her on his floor through their sight-seeing trips of Chicago. Then the romantic dinners, the amazing lovemaking and all the rest of the way to this moment on her porch where her wishes were granted and she had the man of her dreams firmly in her arms.

If this wasn't the handiwork of something extraordinary, she didn't know what was.

"Kismet," she said. "If that means something wonderful then that's exactly what this is."

Merry Christmas, Baby

1

MERRY STUPID CHRISTMAS.

Okay, so Jeannie Carmichael knew that wasn't how the expletive went, but she'd never been one for swearing, even on nights like tonight when she had darn good reason for it.

As the last of the hangers-on began to filter out of the party room, she took a seat and looked over the extent of the work that lay ahead of her. All the snowflakes she'd cheerily hung over the dance floor had to be taken down. Trays of food left behind on the buffet table had to be collected or tossed. Building maintenance had wheeled in cans for depositing trash, but so far, none of the twenty-odd people left at the party seemed to know what to do with them. It seemed as if Jeannie was on her own, left behind to clean up, while the rest of Stryker's employees took their celebrating elsewhere.

And if she received any real thanks for the work, she wouldn't mind it one bit.

Okay, so the occasional employee had tossed out a terse "nice party" here and there. And yes, if her manager, Sabrina, wasn't out on maternity leave or her best friend, Kristin Riley, hadn't gone home sick, they would both be here helping her right now. But that didn't change the fact that every other person at this company—up to and including the senior Mr. Stryker himself—took everything Jeannie did for granted, as if hosting the holiday Christmas party and cleaning up after everyone four hours past her quitting time was a standard part of her job description.

Was it too much to ask that Mr. Stryker could have given her a shout-out during his recognition speech? A simple "Thanks, Jeannie, for arranging things" would have done. That was all. She wasn't asking for a trip to Maui or a gift card or a double-digit pay raise. Just the acknowledgment that he knew she actually existed and that her work was as valuable to the team as everyone else's.

She slumped back in her chair and fought off tears. It was a good thing the bar had closed. She was in the mood to drown her sorrows, and not being one for handling alcohol well, she knew that would have ended badly if she'd been given the opportunity. Besides, she had this place to clean up, and since there weren't any Christmas elves here to do it for her, she'd best get started.

"For someone who's dressed so festively, you don't appear to have enjoyed the party."

The voice belonged to that strange Santa Claus, the one she'd been trying to catch up with all night. On several occasions throughout the evening she'd spotted him across the room chatting with someone, but every time Jeannie tried to corner him, the man magically disappeared. It was an oddity that had constantly bugged her, and she opened her mouth, intending to finally ask him what he was doing here and who invited him—if anyone invited him at all. But then she surveyed the mess in front of her while another handful of employees casually stepped out the door and she decided that at this point, it really didn't matter. The party was over, no harm had been done, and by now even her curiosity had fizzled along with her mood.

Instead, she simply sighed and agreed. "Not really, no."

He shook his head sympathetically. "It's not right to feel low over the holidays. Christmas is a time for cheer." He handed her a candy cane. "Tell me what would take your dim spirit and make it bright."

"Some appreciation would be nice," she grumbled. "But I doubt that's in your bag."

He made a tsk-tsk sound that strangely made her feel slightly better, if not at least understood.

"The gift of human behavior," he mused. "It's the most difficult gift of all. Not as easy as making a toy train or sewing a football. Yet as we age, it's what we learn to cherish most. World peace, the kindness of strangers, charity, true love—they're things that come from the heart, not the hand."

Oookay. "So you're telling me I'm out of luck."

He rolled with jolly laughter and patted her on the shoulder. "You can't change everyone around you, but if you keep your heart open, you might find that special someone who will stick by you and make the rest of the world bearable."

With a wink, the man turned and walked out the door, leaving Jeannie still sitting there grumpy and down, but now in the added state of total confusion.

What was that all about? Keep her heart open? Her heart was already open. And she had plenty of people in her life who stuck by her. It was just that none of them were here right now, that was all.

Shaking her head, she got up and started clearing the tables. Maybe that was what he was trying to tell her, that she should focus on the people who truly mattered and let the rest of them go. For sure, her manager, Sabrina, appreciated her. And here at work, that was what really should count, right? And maybe that was why Jeannie was so down tonight. Her boss had been on leave for weeks, not here to give her the morale boosts she'd grown accustomed to. Add to that her parents' announcement that they were canceling their traditional Christmas Eve dinner—thereby leaving Jeannie with nowhere to go—and it was no wonder she felt neglected and undervalued this holiday season. Who wouldn't feel a little abandoned if put in her shoes?

Her mood validated—if not improved—she spent the next hour straightening up before heading out for the weekend. It had been a long, hectic week getting ready for this celebration and she figured what she really needed was two days away from it all doing something besides thinking about work. Surely, with this project behind her a couple days of rest and relaxation would put her in a better frame of mind.

UNFORTUNATELY, WHEN MONDAY morning rolled around, Jeannie wasn't any less upset. In fact, instead of simply being angry about the party, she'd spent two days brooding about all the other ways the employees at Stryker took advantage of her. She'd racked up such a list of grievances, that by the time she walked into the office, her shoulders were sagged and she felt tired and beaten. Thus, she'd barely noticed the excited grin on Kristin's face as she walked past the woman's cubicle.

"What took you so long to get here?" Kristin asked as she rushed into the aisle as Jeannie passed. "I've been waiting for an hour to find out where these came from!"

Jeannie checked her watch. "Where *what* came from? I'm always here at eight, and—" She glanced down to see that Kristin was wearing a new pair of pretty plum-colored heels. Kristin had a thing for shoes, which made Jeannie wonder if she'd really been sick Friday or if there'd simply been a sale uptown she couldn't miss.

"Are those new?" she asked.

Kristin's blue eyes glimmered. "They're Louis Vuitton."

"Louis who?" To Jeannie, if they weren't sold at the Shoe Mart, they didn't exist.

Kristin waved her off. "Forget the shoes. Come read the card. I'm dying to know who brought you the flowers!"

It was only when they rounded the corner that Jeannie spotted the large bouquet.

She gasped.

Sitting on her desk was a beautiful crystal vase filled with long-stem white carnations and a single plump red rose in the center. The arrangement was huge, consuming half her desk, and tucked underneath it was a small red envelope with her name on it.

"Where did this come from?" she asked.

"I don't know. They were here when I got in." Kristin was nearly bouncing with excitement in her new purple shoes. "Read the card! I've been waiting forever."

A smile formed on Jeannie's lips as she pulled out the card and opened the envelope. Only once in her life had she gotten flowers and those were from her aunt and uncle when she graduated college. They'd been sunflowers— bright, cheery and congratulatory.

These had a different connotation—one entirely romantic—and as she tugged the small card from the envelope, she wondered who in the world could have sent them.

In every crowd there's one who stands out, the card read. *You're the rose in my garden.*

That was it. There was no signature or other identifier that would let her know who had bought them.

She handed the card to Kristin.

"You have a new man in your life?" Kristin gushed. "Why didn't you tell me? This is huge."

Jeannie admitted it would have been huge if it were true. She hadn't gone on a date since her boyfriend, Bryce, dumped her for one of his coworkers at the magazine where he worked. That had been months ago.

"The only man in my life is Arnie," Jeannie said, referring to her beagle.

Kristin's excitement bubbled over. "You have a secret admirer. Oh, this is so romantic."

Jeannie eyed the flowers and grinned. "It is, isn't it?"

"And whoever it is, he really wants you. Chad used to do things like this before we were married. It's how I knew he was serious."

Jeannie stuck her nose in the big bouquet and drank in the fragrant scent of carnations. This had to be the sweetest thing that ever happened to her. For sure, it extinguished her simmering grudge over the Christmas party and the upcoming holiday. If her mystery man had hoped to brighten her mood, he couldn't have picked a better time.

"Who do you think it is?" she wondered aloud.

"It has to be someone who works here. I came in at seven and these were already on your desk. That's way too early for a florist delivery."

Immediately, Jeannie pulled up a mental list of all the single men in the company, but on first thought, no one person popped to the top.

"What about Jerry in Tax?" Kristin asked.

Jeannie crinkled her nose. Jerry was nice, but definitely not her type. She dearly hoped it wasn't him.

"Ooh, what if it's Dirk Holley?" Kristin continued in a low teasing voice.

"Yeah, right." Jeannie rolled her eyes. "I'm hardly *his* type."

Kristin laughed. "You could be. You just have to trade in your cardigan sweaters for red leather pants and tube tops."

"And a boob job," Jeannie whispered. Giggling, she glanced around in fear that someone might have heard, but it was still early and the floor was mostly empty. Not many employees came in before eight-thirty or nine, which Jeannie realized could work in her favor. Whoever left her the beautiful flowers would have to be in the group of people already here. That would narrow down the list of possibilities for sure.

She looked left then right, surveying as much of the office as she could from her desk, but it was hard. The area was a maze of cubicles, enclosed offices and partitions, and she couldn't take in much of the floor without physically wandering the aisles.

"We need to know who this is," Kristin said, still studying the card in her hand. Like Jeannie, she began looking around as if hoping to find their mystery man peeking over a cubicle wall.

"I know, but how?"

TROY HUTCHINS STOOD AROUND the corner and listened as Jeannie and Kristin contemplated who had brought the flowers. His heart was beating fast. His palms were damp and clammy. When he'd read the funny little pamphlet that Santa Claus had given him at the party Friday night, the steps titled "How To Get The Girl" seemed fun and easy. And when the man had guaranteed that by following them Troy would win over Jeannie's affections, he figured what did he have to lose? For sure, his own efforts to get her attention had failed. So when the odd man offered advice, Troy decided to take it.

Only now, with the first move made, he was having his

doubts. The two women were tossing out names, Jeannie shooting several of them down, and not once had either of them mentioned him. He wasn't sure if that was good or bad. What he did know was that this had to work, because for the entire year that he'd worked for Stryker & Associates he'd wanted Jeannie so badly it hurt.

He remembered the day he first saw her sitting at her desk sorting papers, so pretty with her friendly blue eyes and long blond hair. She'd been humming, her voice sweet as a songbird, and when she'd caught his eye and smiled, her sunny expression shot an arrow through his heart that was still stuck there today.

He'd spent the next twelve months learning as much as he could about her. He'd wallowed in grief when he found out she had a boyfriend then hollered with joy when the fool broke up with her. And since that time, he'd been trying to determine the best way to ask her out. He'd almost come straight out and asked her the very day he'd found out she was single, but she'd fended him off before he'd gotten the chance. She was still crushed from the breakup, in denial that maybe the loser that left her would change his mind and come back. And though Troy knew the guy didn't deserve her grief or her heart, he was forced to back off until she got over him.

Instead, he bided his time as her platonic friend in IT, storing up a mental list of her likes and dislikes and falling further and further in love as he did. He learned what made her laugh and what made her mad, how she liked to spend her spare time and what she hoped for her future. He knew she preferred dogs over cats, sherbet over ice cream and burgers over steak. She liked country-western music and movies with happy endings. He knew about the scar on her knee from when she slipped on gravel as a kid, that she was the baby in a family of five, and that one day she wanted to travel to Scotland to track down her family's ancestry. He knew everything about her, including the fact that she was officially over the ex-boyfriend who'd broken her heart and that she was ready for romance again.

And Troy wasn't going to miss his opportunity a second time.

He'd tried to ask her on a date at the party Friday night, thinking the mood would be ripe. Only Jeannie was so distracted with all the arrangements, he'd quickly recognized that it wasn't the place. That was when that quirky Santa Claus had approached him and asked him what he most wanted for Christmas. And when Troy pointed to Jeannie and confessed his aching heart, the man had handed him the glossy pamphlet.

Troy had to admit, it was a strange encounter, one he would have dismissed if it weren't for the interesting suggestions on the page. It was almost as if it had been written just for him, and since he hadn't considered the idea of a slow seduction before, he decided to give it a try.

"What about Troy Hutchins?" he heard Kristin ask.

He froze as he awaited the answer, hoping for the best and fearing the worst. What if she laughed? What if she brushed him off as not her type like she'd done with Jerry in Tax? It would ruin him, and the thought of it almost had him turning down the hall before she answered, not wanting to hear the bad news if that was what it would be.

Then he heard her reply, "Troy?" and his feet rooted into place.

She paused as if she were considering, and the infinitesimal seconds seemed to roll on like hours until he finally heard her say, "This seems awfully romantic for Troy. I have a hard time picturing him as a flowers kind of guy."

And that was it. They moved onto other names, leaving Troy to ponder how he felt about that remark. Okay, so it wasn't bad. She hadn't shot him down or crushed his hopes by scoffing off the idea of him being her mystery man, which meant the door was still wide open for step two on the list.

And as for her assumption that he wasn't romantic, well, apparently in all Troy's efforts to get to know Jeannie, she hadn't gotten to know him as well in return. But if things went his way that would all change—very soon—and Jeannie Carmichael would find out exactly how romantic he could be.

2

JEANNIE SPENT THE entire morning trying to work but instead spent it staring at the beautiful bouquet on her desk and wondering who was responsible. She'd hoped by now someone would have claimed it, and every time a male coworker passed her desk, she froze, wondering if it was him and how she would feel if it was.

Though she wasn't getting much work done, she had to admit the experience was exciting. Somewhere on the floor was a man who wanted her affections, a very kind and creative man who was putting a lot of effort into getting them. And speculating who it might be was both fun and unnerving.

Throughout the day, all of Operations had gotten in on it, trying to guess who they thought it might be. Jeannie had a fairly significant list of candidates and a number of people felt certain they knew who it was, but each of them named someone different. It had become the buzz of the floor, but by quitting time, no one had come forward and she was forced to go home and spend the night in wonder.

The next morning, she came in to find her desk exactly as she'd left it the night before. Nothing new had arrived, and for the bulk of the morning, she began to fear that maybe her secret admirer had gotten cold feet. Maybe the flowers had been it and there would be nothing more, or worse, maybe it had been someone's cruel joke to tease her. She had a hard time believing *that* was true, but with the hours ticking by and nothing surfacing, she couldn't help the worried thoughts.

Until she returned from lunch to find a frosty bottle of her favorite orange soda sitting on her desk next to a bag of peanut M&M's. The accompanying note read, *If you'll let me, I'll make sure your days are filled with sweetness.*

A tiny thrill sped up Jeannie's spine. So it hadn't been a joke, and her mystery man was still quite alive and well. But now the question of who he was began to truly burn.

"He doesn't just work here, he really *knows* you," Kristin observed, hovering over and reading the card just like she'd done the day before.

Kristin was right. Whoever left this for her knew that orange soda and peanut M&Ms were her standard mid-afternoon treats, the quick sugar fix that picked her up and kept her going until quitting time. He'd even gotten the brand of soda right, which wasn't easy since there was only one shop down in the lobby that sold it.

"'If you'll let me,'" she repeated, studying the words he'd written. "How can I let him if I don't know who he is?"

"He's torturing you. He's torturing us both," Kristin said.

And she was right. By the end of the day Tuesday, there'd been nothing more and Jeannie was forced to go home once again no closer to knowing who her admirer was. Yet the next morning, another new surprise waited for her. She'd come in to find all her filing had been done and a large copy job she'd had on her desk was completed. The card read, *I'm willing to help so you can spend your nights with me.*

And with each gesture, her list of candidates changed. She and Kristin and several other coworkers kept adding and dropping men from the list based on each new surprise. A number of them had gone out and cornered a few suspects, asking point-blank if they were Jeannie's secret admirer. Though no one could conclusively figure out who it could be. And by Wednesday night, Jeannie was getting worried again. Thursday was the last day at the office before the Christmas weekend, and the thought of having to spend the holiday still in the dark over the identity of her mystery man was too much to bear. This waiting was killing her, the constant speculation snatching the sleep from her nights. If she had to continue through the holiday, she'd be ruined.

Fortunately, she didn't have to. When she came in Thursday morning, she found a single red rose on her desk with the note, *You've heard my offers, now meet the man. I'll be downstairs at the coffee shop holding a rose like this one. I'll see you at noon.*

Immediately, she trembled with both excitement and nerves. She'd finally get to meet her mystery man, but would that be good or bad? What if it was someone she truly had no interest in? It was a question she'd asked herself dozens of times since Monday morning, but now the reality of it was close enough to touch. How would she handle it? What would she say?

On the flipside, there were a few men she was privately rooting for. Brad Buckingham in Product Management had topped her list, though admittedly, she barely knew him. But he was the type—tall and dreamy—that could pique her interest easily. She'd watched him give a presentation at a quarterly meeting earlier in the year and had loved his casual confidence. He'd been funny and bold, the knight-inshining-armor type that Jeannie had always thought would complement her quiet nature.

Then there was Carlos in Maintenance, not an employee of Stryker but a contractor for the building who spent plenty of time in their offices. Carlos was born in Honduras and Jeannie had always loved his Latin accent and dark fiery eyes. Over the past few days, she'd all but mentally turned him into Zorro, her masked fantasy lover who could sweep her off her feet and fight off evil for her love.

They were silly fantasies that had made her giggle, but now that she held an invitation in her hand the whole thing became a serious matter. If the man was someone she genuinely liked, this could be the wonderful start of something new. But if it was someone she really wasn't interested in…

She didn't want to think about that. Instead, she tucked the card in her purse and checked the clock. She had four hours to agonize over it. And she didn't doubt they would be the longest four hours of her life.

"I DON'T WANT TO GO," Jeannie confessed. Clutching her purse to her chest, she eyed the clock as the second hand ticked and ticked. It was three minutes to noon. Her pulse raced and her throat was tight with angst.

"You have to go. We've been waiting all week," Kristin urged.

"What if it's Jerry from Tax?"

She'd been preparing that speech since this morning, the one that appreciated his efforts but let him down gently, and she knew when it came to actually delivering it, she'd blow it completely. She knew she was too soft to let down anyone who had gone through such considerate efforts to win her over, and she'd end up on a date no matter what happened today.

"What if it's Brad Buckingham?" Kristin countered.

That lifted Jeannie's spirits slightly, but didn't completely calm her jitters. She'd noted that it had been over a year since she'd been on a first date, and even that had been a foursome with mutual friends who had fixed her up with Bryce. This was territory she hadn't treaded in ages, if not ever.

"I can't do this."

"Yes, you can." Kristin rose from her chair, took Jeannie by the shoulders and led her to the elevators. "Just go down there, see who it is and then go from there. You'll be fine, don't worry."

Sucking in a needy breath, Jeannie waited for the doors to open then stepped inside.

"Then hurry back up and tell us who it is!" Kristin called as the elevator doors closed between them.

Where the four-hour wait to get to this moment had seemed like a million years, now the elevator was zipping her downstairs and depositing her in the lobby in record time. And with hesitant steps she made her way to the coffee shop, pausing outside for one more final gulp of air before she stepped through the doors.

And when she did, she caught her first sight of the man who had been tormenting her with romantic gestures all week long.

Troy.

The breath she'd been holding escaped her and she found herself alternately pleased and disappointed. It wasn't Jerry from Tax, but it wasn't Brad or Carlos, either. It was Troy, one of the last people she'd expected. Okay, so he'd made the list once or twice, but she'd kept dismissing him, not just because she hadn't considered him a romantic, but also because she'd presumed him too painfully shy for such grand gestures.

Walking toward his table, she recalled the first time she'd met him. He'd come to her desk to check out a problem with her computer. From the start, she'd noticed his gentle voice and those hypnotizing blue eyes, but she'd barely been able to talk to him. He'd been so nervous his hands had shaken, and when he talked he'd stumbled over his words. She'd been afraid to do much more than say please and thank you for fear that she'd make him feel worse.

Granted, over time he'd eased up and they'd become quite friendly, but as she neared his table and he stood, she could see the shy, hesitant man had returned.

He held out the red rose, the flower trembling in his hand, and though he looked terrified, the affection in those midnight-blue eyes was unmistakable.

"Are you surprised it's me?" he asked.

"Yes," she admitted, accepting the rose and taking a seat.

The nervous smile disappeared from his face. "That's not a bad thing, is it?"

"No! Of course not. It's a good thing. All your gifts and gestures have been so sweet, and—" Jeannie started babbling just like she knew she would, and she didn't doubt that by the end of this visit, she would end up accepting a date with Troy, too soft and kindhearted to turn him down.

But that was okay, because this was Troy, her friend from IT. She could go on a date with Troy and maybe even have some fun. Right?

3

TROY HAD TO ADMIT THAT he'd hoped for a brighter smile when Jeannie walked into the coffee shop and spotted him as the man behind her gifts. In fact, for a minute there he feared she was going to give him a thanks-but-no-thanks speech that he hadn't prepared for at all. But once she sat down and started talking, he realized she wasn't intending to bolt, and it eased the fears that had taken him over.

"Really, thank you," she said for about the fourth time. "Your gifts were so thoughtful and they made my week."

He watched as she nervously toyed with the rose and it bothered him. He didn't want Jeannie to feel awkward around him. This was supposed to advance their friendship, not ruin it. But he supposed he had just changed the dynamics of their relationship in the course of one moment. It had taken him most of the year to establish himself as her friendly acquaintance. Now he wanted her to think of him as a potential lover, and he had to accept that it could take some adjustment.

But that was okay. He was a patient man and he had a plan. This week had been about getting her attention and making her think about him in a way other than Troy, that quiet guy from IT. Now he needed to show her what he already knew—that if she gave him a chance, she'd find out how right they could be together.

"I'm glad you liked them," he said, then watched with concern as she chewed her lip and fumbled.

Reaching across the table, he placed his hand over hers, the simple touch zipping through him with the realization that it was the first time he'd actually had a hand on her.

It felt good. Really good. More would feel even better. But he could already see that wasn't going to happen if she didn't stop fretting.

"Jeannie," he began, "don't feel pressured. I want to take you on a date. I've wanted to for a long time. All I'm asking is that you give it some thought. If the answer ends up being no, I'll respect that, and we'll go back to business as usual."

Okay, so that last part was a lie. Pretty much, if she turned him down, he'd be crushed and humiliated, but she didn't need to know that. Right now, she only needed to know that he was the same guy she'd gotten to know this last year. Nothing had changed that.

Sliding his hand away, he picked up the menus and handed her one, noting that some of the calm was returning to her face. "In the meantime, will you have lunch with me? I'd love to hear about your plans for the holidays."

After a long pause an easy smile formed on her face and she nodded. "Okay. That sounds great."

She accepted the menu and he quickly went to task turning the conversation to the casual chitchat they'd enjoyed a number of times before. "So does your family do anything special for Christmas?"

She huffed. "We used to, but not this year." As they perused the menus she told him about her family's tradition that began on Christmas Eve with a casual dinner of homemade pizzas then stretched through Christmas Day, where they gathered with the extended family over a large holiday dinner at her grandmother's house.

"We're still doing the big dinner Christmas Day," she explained. "But my parents are canceling Christmas Eve. My brother and sister are both married, so they're juggling dual families now, and everyone decided that it would be easier if we skipped Christmas Eve and simply focused on the big dinner."

"You look disappointed."

She shrugged. "I understand. With my brother and sister spending Christmas Eve with their in-laws, it would have just been me and my parents. And since they're invited every year to a big party at my father's lodge, they decided to do that instead."

"What are you going to do?"

"Stay home with Arnie, I guess." She rolled her eyes and shook her head. "I'm sorry. I'm sitting here complaining and I really shouldn't. It's just been kind of a disappointing week." Then she gave him a genuine smile. "Which was why the flowers and notes were so sweet."

Now it was her turn to reach out and take his hand. "I know I keep saying it, but you picked a wonderful week to cheer me up. I really appreciate it."

He'd love to cheer her up every day if she'd let him, and he'd nearly opened his mouth and spouted as much. But his better judgment told him not to go too fast.

"I'm glad. You deserve cheering up," he simply said.

The server came to take their order and he wasn't surprised when Jeannie addressed the woman by name. It was one of the things he adored about her, that she took an interest in everyone and always made a point to be kind. Jeannie was the type who left a bright spot everywhere she went, warming the office with her sunny smile and cheery sweaters. It was why it pained him to see her so disappointed about Christmas. She brought so much light to everyone around her. This should be the season to get it back. She only needed someone to do that for her.

"So what about you?" she asked. "What do you do for the holidays?"

"My parents' neighbors are having a party tomorrow night. Then this year, the family's gathering at my brother's for Christmas." He shrugged. "It's nothing special. To tell you the truth, it's just good being home for the holidays again."

She looked puzzled. "Why? Were you gone?"

"I spent eight years in the army, the last two of them in Afghanistan. This is my second Christmas back home, but I don't think I'll ever stop appreciating it."

"I had no idea you were military." She blinked. "Wow."

Her charmed expression took on a glimmer of attraction he'd never seen directed his way before. Apparently, his army career scored some serious bonus points. Heck, if he'd known that, he would have mentioned it a long time ago.

"That's such an honorable thing to do," she went on. "Especially being in a war like we are."

"It was more selfish than that," he confessed, probably to his own disadvantage. A more calculating man would have run with it and gotten the girl by claiming to be a patriotic war hero. Unfortunately, Troy's unpretentious nature rarely offered anything but raw honesty. "I wanted a career in computers and that seemed the best way for me to go about it."

She smiled and studied him before finally saying, "It fits. I've always seen you as very quiet and shy, but that's not right." She nodded as she spoke. "You're one of those reserved military men. The strong, silent type—it makes so much more sense."

If it kept the twinkle in her eye, she could believe whatever she wanted. Granted, he had gained a layer of discipline from the army, but he had always been a quiet man, especially in crowds. And as for shy, well, even the army hadn't helped him get over his terror of pretty women—at least, the ones he was deeply attracted to.

Sure, he'd been around the block and had managed just fine. But every now and then, he'd run in to that special someone who made him stupid and turned his tongue in knots—like, for instance, a sunny blonde with a spine-tingling smile, angelic blue eyes and perky snowflake earrings.

It had always been his curse, and it was an embarrassing curse to have. He could walk down a dark alley in the worst section of Chicago without flinching. But get him near a woman like Jeannie and he became a stumbling bundle of nerves.

"I hope that's a good thing," he said.

"It is. I'm enjoying learning about you." Their lunch arrived, and after she settled and started to eat, she went on. "So tell me more about yourself. How do you spend your weekends?"

"That depends. If it's hockey season, I spend them cheering. If it's baseball season, I spend them crying in my beer."

She laughed. "You're a Cubbies fan."

He placed his hand over his heart. "With all its pain and agony."

She told him she was a Cubs fan, too, but he already knew that. It was one of the many things he'd noticed over the past year that kept convincing him that she was the woman of his dreams. It hadn't simply been her looks, her bright disposition or her kind heart. They also had a number of things in common, and a love of baseball was one of them.

The conversation moved on to New Year's and work and what was on their Christmas lists, and by the time they were done with lunch any remnant of tension between them had vanished. It felt like a good thing, but he couldn't be sure. Regardless, he had come to a point where he could do nothing more in terms of advances. This meeting had been the last item on that Santa's list and now Troy would find out whether or not the old man's plan worked. Troy had laid his cards on the table, had handed Jeannie his heart and could only wait to see if she accepted it or graciously handed it back. He prayed it was the former, feared it might be the latter, but mostly, he hated that he'd come to the end of the line.

If she turned him down, he had to accept it, and the finality left him feeling totally exposed—a state he hadn't anticipated when he'd started down this path. But as they left the restaurant and took the elevator back up to their office, he discovered he wasn't going to have to stay in limbo for long.

Turning and smiling, Jeannie looked up at him and uttered, "Yes."

He blinked. "Yes?"

"In answer to your question, I would love to go out with you on a date."

He almost thought he'd imagined the words, that his desire had been so great he'd fabricated it. But then she pulled out a notepad, jotted down her address and phone number and handed it to him, and when he touched the paper he knew it was real.

"You would?"

"I would." Then as the elevator doors opened, she grinned brightly and said, "I'm looking forward to it."

4

IT WAS CHRISTMAS EVE DAY and Jeannie was home alone as she'd expected, but instead of feeling lonely and depressed, her thoughts were consumed by Troy.

Yesterday she'd been so surprised that he was her secret admirer, but the more she reflected over the past year, the more it began to make sense. Troy had always been so quiet, so subtle in his approach that she'd missed the signs that seemed obvious now. At company functions, he'd always somehow ended up at her table. She was the one he'd ask to test new hardware. He got his morning coffee about the same time she did and went to the same deli for lunch. For a year, the man must have gone through painstaking efforts to get close, and all that time, his attempts had gone unnoticed.

Shamefully, Jeannie had to admit that he'd simply never caught her attention. Her eye had always been turned to the talkative types, the extroverts who spoke up in meetings and cracked jokes in crowds. Her fantasy man had been the bold superhero, the swashbuckler or the suave sophisticate. But after this week of steamy surprises, she was beginning to uncover a desire for the strong quiet types, too.

She'd spent half the night awake in bed thinking about

Troy. With his short dark hair and sapphire eyes, she hadn't dismissed him romantically for lacking sex appeal. On the contrary, he had some very fine features bundled up in that serious physique. She recalled the annual picnic last summer when he'd swapped his normal loose-fitting shirts for a snug T-shirt. She'd been impressed with a pair of biceps that appeared to get plenty of work. In fact, she remembered musing that the man definitely didn't spend his life in front of a computer given his broad muscled chest and tight round butt.

But just then Nick Castle had waltzed up, flashed his million-dollar smile and told her she looked pretty as a spring garden in her flowery skirt and she'd forgotten all about Troy.

And that was how it went. Whenever Troy quietly caught her attention, something louder pulled it away.

But she wasn't forgetting him now. Lying in the dark last night, she'd mentally gone over every inch of him, from his short cropped hair down his long lean frame and back up to the bashful smile that now seemed pretty sexy. She wondered what his lips would feel like on hers. Would his kisses be gentle or would he surprise her with deep commanding passion? She'd fantasized about it both ways and found she'd like either to be the case. She wondered what those hands would feel like against her skin, how that sultry gaze might look under the dim lights of a romantic restaurant, or how his deep voice might sound between the sheets.

By the wee hours of the morning, she'd fully worked herself into a state of lust and excitement. Then she doused it with fears that she might be mistaking appreciation for genuine interest. Without a doubt, this had been the single most romantic thing that had ever happened to her, and she couldn't help the fear that she might be more intrigued by the gestures than the man. Several times, she'd told herself that wasn't the case, but in truth, it was a question she wouldn't be able to answer until she spent more time with him. And that wouldn't start until she went back to work on Monday.

Oh, it was going to be a long weekend.

Sighing, she checked her watch and saw that it was barely noon. She had a long way to go before they were back at the office. It would seem even longer if she spent the day before Christmas sitting on the couch daydreaming and speculating. What she needed to do was put it out of her head for a while and go on with her holiday weekend. She pushed up from the couch and stepped to the window to check the weather—a move that got Arnie's attention. Quickly, her old dog shuffled off his bed and hobbled to the door. Arnie knew every sign that pointed to a walk, and he was always ready to go. Right now, Jeannie thought that maybe some cool air would do her good.

"Do you want to go out and brave the elements, Arnie?"

The dog barked.

"Well, if you can, I can, too." She grabbed her boots and jacket then went for Arnie's leash. "There's no sense in spending my Christmas agonizing over a man I won't see for three days." She snapped the leash on his collar, but just as she was preparing to leave the phone rang. Moving to pick it up, she was both surprised and pleased to discover it was Troy.

"Hi, Troy," she said, her mood quickly perking.

"Hi, um—" he cleared his throat "—I was wondering if you could use a Christmas tree."

"A Christmas tree?"

"They were letting them go cheap at the lot this morning so I picked up an extra."

She blinked. "You bought me a tree?"

"Yep."

A smile slowly formed on her lips. "That's crazy."

And completely adorable.

"Probably. I'm in the neighborhood, though, so if you'd like it I could drop it by."

She checked what she was wearing, frumpy sweats and wooly socks. She'd showered, but she was hardly presentable. She wondered how much time she had to dot on some makeup and change into jeans.

"How close are you?"

Her doorbell rang. "Close."

"That's you, isn't it?"

"Yep."

Still holding the phone in her hand, she stepped to the entry and opened the door to find Troy standing there with a bushy evergreen in one hand and a shopping bag in the other. He wore a dark navy peacoat with a matching knit cap pulled low over his head, and with a light flush of cold coloring his cheeks, he looked as sexy as a magazine model. It brought her attention back to her own dire appearance.

"I'm sorry, I wasn't expecting company," she said. "I'm not exactly dressed appropriately."

Those blue eyes scanned her from head to toe. "You look beautiful, Jeannie."

He'd said it with such open sincerity that she genuinely believed him. Instead of the typical suave attempt at flattery, Troy's matter-of-fact observation seemed to come straight from the heart. And it hit hers square in the center.

"Well, come in." She backed up and pulled the leash off Arnie. Their walk was officially canceled, though

Arnie didn't seem to mind. Something more exciting had shown up.

The tree still propped in one hand, Troy bent down to pet the dog. "Hey, buddy boy." Arnie became an instant fan. "You're an old guy, aren't you?"

"I found him at the shelter five years ago," Jeannie explained. "I'd gone to look at some puppies, but when I got there Arnie gave me the look."

Troy nodded. "I know that look."

"Do you have a dog?"

"An Irish setter, but he's still with my folks." He stood up and eyed the room. "So where should we put this?"

"How about the corner by the window? I can move the chair to the spare bedroom."

After fetching the stand from his truck, he went to work setting up the tree while Jeannie started a pot of coffee.

"Can you stay and help me decorate it? I've put on coffee and I've got stuff for sandwiches in the fridge."

"I'd love to."

He pulled off his cap and shrugged out of his coat, revealing that sexy upper body she'd admired back at the summer picnic. Seeing him again in worn jeans and a T-shirt, she confirmed that the attraction she'd felt through the night most definitely wasn't misguided appreciation. The man had a seriously nice body. She only wondered why she'd so easily let a smooth compliment distract her from it. Obviously, when it came to men, Jeannie had a few lessons to learn.

They spent the next few hours working on the tree while listening to holiday music and sharing their Christmas traditions. And the more she continued to learn about Troy, the more smitten she became.

She eyed him as he cut strips of color paper for the garland they were making. The image took on a new dose of sweetness when she considered that just two years ago he was in a combat area overseas. Now he was sitting on her living-room floor doing the childlike task of making paper garland, all the while acting like he was genuinely having a good time.

She studied him then looked up at the tree. "That tree wasn't on sale, was it?"

"Nope," he casually replied without so much as looking up from his cuttings.

"You bought it as an excuse to come over."

He shrugged. "You said yesterday that it wasn't going to seem like Christmas." He looked up at the tree, the white lights twinkling behind a mix of ornaments that were half store-bought and half concocted from things she had around her house. "Now it seems like Christmas."

And for Troy, it was just that simple. She'd complained and he'd come to fix it. She got the impression if she asked for the world he'd find a way to hand that over, too.

"Troy Hutchins, you're the loveliest man I know."

He slid her a glance and winked. "I am a catch. I'm glad it hasn't taken you long to see that."

She giggled. "Yes, I pick up on things pretty quickly."

And that included the fact that if she didn't take this man's affections seriously, she was the biggest idiot in the world.

Her midnight fantasies came back to her full swing as she took in that subtle mouth and wondered what he could do with it. She ached to settle the debate over what kind of kisser he was, though by this point, she barely cared. If he didn't kiss well, she'd teach him how and enjoy every minute in training. It was the soul one couldn't change, and Jeannie wasn't sure she'd ever met a better one. For sure, she doubted she'd ever meet someone like him again.

"I also think you didn't come over just to drink coffee

and make paper Christmas decorations," she said, putting down her paper chain and scooting a little closer.

She caught his freshly showered scent and it smelled good. She wanted to kiss him and knew without a doubt that if it was going to happen, it would have to be her move. And that alone was rather exciting. Jeannie had never been the seductress before. She'd always let the man take the lead. But given that it had taken Troy this long to simply make his interest known, she wasn't going to wait on him to make a pass to get her into bed. That could be months.

She watched a hard swallow roll down his throat as his eyes dropped down to her chest. She wished she wasn't wearing her frumpy sweatshirt. The view would have been so much more enticing if she'd slipped on something a little revealing, but the hungry look on his face said it didn't really matter. His mind was going where hers was already waiting.

"I came to spend time doing anything you want to do," he said, his gaze sliding down farther.

She took the scissors and set them on the table, then guided his big hand up under her sweatshirt and placed it on her breast. "I'd like to do something like this," she whispered, moving her lips close to his where all he had to do was turn his head to kiss her.

A dark fire smoothed over his gaze as he palmed her breast and let out a slow sigh. "We could do this," he uttered hoarsely. Then without waiting for another advance, he tugged her onto his lap, cupped her cheek with his hand and smothered her mouth with his.

5

Troy took Jeannie in his arms and tried to remember a time when he'd wanted something so badly. For months, he'd ached and pined and daydreamed, first waiting for her to be available then strategizing the best way to get her right here in this spot. And now that he had what he wanted and his fantasy was real in his arms, he had no idea where to start.

He drew her mouth to his and got his first taste, sweet just like he'd expected. It took all his restraint to kiss her gently, to take his time, to hold back, when his body begged him to devour and possess. With hands nearly trembling with need, he smoothed them over her breasts and down her waist. She felt exactly as he'd imagined, soft and tender, the way he'd always liked a woman. And it was just another arrow in his heart.

He'd been in love with Jeannie since the first day they met. She'd stolen his heart and now she was here offering him the most intimate part of her soul. He only prayed that for her this wasn't simply a fling. He didn't think it was. He didn't picture Jeannie as the type to casually take a lover then move on the next day, and the fact that she was here, spreading her body for him, had to mean he'd done his job in stealing her affections.

He hoped so, because he knew once this night was over there would be no going back. He loved her deeply, wanted her badly, and once he got inside retreat wouldn't be an option.

She groaned and splayed her hands over his shoulders as she pressed her bottom against his erection. "I think we should move this to the bedroom," she suggested, sending a pulse of fire through his veins.

The words were music to his ears, exactly what he'd dreamed of hearing for months, but despite himself, he couldn't go forward with this unless she truly understood.

Cupping her face in his hands, he looked into those beautiful blue eyes and confessed, "I want that more than anything, but you have to understand, Jeannie. For me, this isn't casual."

Some of the heat drained from her gaze and she blinked. "I didn't think it was."

"So if you don't feel you're ready for all this, I think we need to slow down."

His body cursed him and his heart stopped beating while he watched her expression and waited for her reply. It was agony knowing he could take her right now without thought for tomorrow, but he knew this had to be said. Because no matter how wonderful a weekend in Jeannie's bed would be, it wouldn't match the heartache of having her only to discover that this would be a one-time thing.

Slowly a smile formed on her face. "I couldn't make love to a man I wasn't serious about."

"I'm sorry," he quickly said. "I didn't mean to insinuate—"

She pressed a finger to his lips and shushed him. "I'd

be a fool to let a wonderful man like you slip through my fingers." Her smile widened. "I'd like to be your girlfriend. I want to be your lover. And spend the time finding out if we could be something more."

"Oh, Jeannie," he said, pulling her mouth to his and drinking in those beautiful words. He ached to tell her how much he loved her, but he knew it was too much too soon. So instead, he scooped her up and took her to bed, deciding to show her with his hands and body just how deeply his feelings went.

The path to her bedroom felt like miles, and when they finally got there, he let her down and helped her out of her clothes, the pressure building in his loin with every inch of supple skin she exposed. And when she finally shed it all, he stood for a long moment and simply took it in.

"So beautiful," he whispered, placing his hot hands against her waist and taking a bare breast between his lips. She lolled her head to the side and moaned, arching into him, drawing him closer before a shiver ran over her and she sighed.

"You need to come to bed," she said, grabbing his shirt and drawing him toward the big double bed in the center of her room. "I want you naked and inside me."

She wasn't going to have to ask him twice.

BARE, HOT AND READY, Jeannie slipped under the covers as she watched Troy pull off his clothing and expose that glorious body. His wonderful confession in her living room still sounded in her ears, but more touching than the words he'd spoken had been the look in his eyes as he expressed his intentions.

She'd never had a man look at her with such affection, nor had she ever felt in her heart such a deep sense that she'd found something special. As Troy ducked under the covers and covered her body with his, there wasn't a remnant of doubt in her mind that she'd found a man worth pursuing, and that knowledge filled her heart.

"You're so beautiful," he said again, smoothing his hands over her skin and leaving a trail of heat in their wake. And then he went to work filling her body with pleasure.

She drew a shuddering breath as his lips touched her breasts, she gasped when his long fingers slipped up between her legs, and she moaned as he used his hands and lips to coax her toward climax. Every inch of his hard body seduced her, from the firm planes of his chest down to his strong thighs tickling against her toes. And with every touch, she edged closer to bliss.

They took their time stroking and exploring while Christmas music from the living room filled the air, and it wasn't long before they'd found an easy rhythm. He pushed two fingers deep then eased them out, ebbing and arcing, circling and thrusting until she began to squirm in his embrace.

"Yes," he urged, his mouth pressed close to her temple. "Come for me, baby."

And she did, digging her fingers into those strong biceps and circling her calf around his as she pulled him close and drowned her cries in the crook of his neck.

"Oh, yeah," he groaned, the silky lull of his voice spilling like velvet over her skin. "I like you like this." He pressed his lips over her skin, across her shoulder. "Relaxed, pleasured and happy." He moved over her and sank his gaze into hers. "There's nothing more stunning than the look on your face right now."

Then with one smooth move, he sheathed himself and pushed inside.

"Ohhh," Jeannie groaned as his thick length filled her. He moved in one long stroke, filling her deeply until she arched her back to take in more. And as he began working up another climax, she realized that even her fantasies hadn't done justice to the man taking possession of her now.

She'd imagined his gentle touches as well as the commanding force of his thrust. But what she'd missed was that cherished look in his eyes that couldn't be fabricated in her dreams. And as he brought them to the edge and over, that look touched a place that had never felt contact before.

For a long time after, he remained inside, their bodies connected. And when their breathing slowed and she rolled into his arms, she rested her head on his shoulder and sighed.

"I just realized, you're the answer to my Christmas wish," she said.

He tenderly kissed her forehead, as she curled into his embrace. "How's that?"

"Remember that guy at the party last week dressed as Santa Claus?" she asked.

"Sure."

"I eventually caught up to him at the end and had the strangest conversation. I'd been feeling unappreciated, annoyed with the people at work and depressed that my parents had changed their plans for Christmas Eve. And when I said something to that effect, he'd told me that I couldn't control the people around me, but if I was lucky, I could find someone special who would make me feel special."

He stroked his long fingers slowly up her back. "I think that's how love works."

Tipping her chin up, she looked up at him and grinned. "I think he brought me you."

"I'm pretty sure he did," Troy agreed.

Coiling her arm around his waist, she pressed her mouth

to his chest and drank him in, from the true heart behind those ribs to the sexy body wrapped in hers. She couldn't deny that what she was experiencing right now was a gift, and she intended to cherish it for as long as Troy would let her.

"So did you find out where the odd guy came from?" he asked.

"No, I didn't. I never asked. But I've chosen to think he was magic. Maybe even the real Santa Claus."

"I like that."

Then she pulled herself up and kissed Troy, long and deep until they were kissed out and had to come up for air.

"Merry Christmas, baby," Troy said, brushing his nose against hers.

"Yes, it most definitely is."

Epilogue

JEANNIE CARMICHAEL WALKED brusquely toward Wacker Drive with Nick Castle, both having run into each other before work at the same coffee shop, as they sometimes did. It was two weeks after New Year's and the bitter cold of January still hung in the early morning air as they headed for Willis Tower to start their workday.

"So did you enjoy the holidays this year?" Jeannie asked.

"It was great. How about you?"

Jeannie smiled wide. "It was my best Christmas ever."

Nick winked. "I take it our buddy Troy had something to do with that."

Jeannie slid him a glance. She could have made the same comment about he and Allie Madison, considering it was all over the office that the two of them had become an item. But she kept that to herself. Despite the rumors, she got the impression Nick and Allie were trying to keep their new relationship out of the spotlight, at least until they could prove to management that the romance wouldn't get in the way of their jobs. Silly, since no one assumed it would, but given John Jr. had recently announced his resignation and everyone was speculating that Nick might replace him, she could understand their desire to keep their personal lives personal for the time being.

"There's nothing better than spending the holidays with the ones you love," was all she said.

"You've got that right."

As they rounded the corner, they approached Monica Newell heading for the lobby doors.

Nick checked his watch. "It's 7:55, Monica. You keep showing up for work this late, people are going to accuse you of slacking."

Jeannie's eyes widened. Only Nick could get away with making a statement like that to Monica, and even so, Jeannie wondered what kind of snapping remark he'd get back. But to her surprise, Monica actually smiled and laughed.

"All work and no play makes Monica a dull gal, Nick. You know that."

Jeannie blinked. She had to be hearing things, because it sounded like Monica just made a joke.

Then to add to her shock, Monica added, "Good morning, Jeannie." She gestured to Jeannie's scarf. "That's a beautiful scarf. Was that a Christmas present?"

"Uh, yes, yes, it was."

Monica's smile was genuine. "Someone has lovely taste."

"My sister, thanks."

As Nick held open the door, the two women stepped in, Jeannie still in a state wondering what had happened to turn Monica from a chilly ice queen into someone…nice.

"There's our short-timer," Nick said from over her shoulder, and Jeannie looked up to see John Jr. standing at the elevator.

John nodded. "I start the police academy in three weeks."

Nick shook his head. "I still say you're crazy as a loon."

"I don't," Jeannie said. "I think it's great you're pursuing your dream."

John scowled at Nick before turning and grinning at Jeannie. "Thank you, Jeannie. I'm pleased to say that I'm happier than I've ever been."

As the two men entered the elevator, Jeannie mused that she could say the same about herself. And Nick for that matter. In fact, now that she recalled, this wasn't the first time since Christmas that she'd noticed the smile on Monica's face, too. It seemed ever since the holidays, the whole tone at Stryker & Associates had changed. People were more relaxed, were acting kinder to each other, not so pressured and aloof.

Or maybe it was just her imagination. Who knew?

As the elevator doors began to close, a man slipped through and Jeannie immediately recognized him as the peculiar man who had been at their holiday party. Except now he wasn't dressed up like Santa Claus. Today he was wearing a charcoal-gray overcoat and a dark navy suit. His hair was trimmed and his beard was shorter, but Jeannie was positive it was the same man who had entertained at their party all night.

And apparently, she wasn't the only one who thought so.

As the old man hit the elevator button, Nick said, "Hey, Claus, I didn't know you worked in this building."

The man regarded Nick curiously. "The name's Simonson, not Claus, but yes, my business has been in this building for a number of years."

Nick chuckled. "Okay, but you're the guy who was at our party last month. You were dressed in that fancy red suit and handing out candy canes."

Mr. Simonson laughed with the same jolly ho-ho-ho they'd all heard before. "I'm afraid my company is too busy for parties during the holiday season. We have our annual celebration in the spring after the rush."

"No, not your party, ours. Stryker & Associates? The big conference room upstairs? We had the music and the eats and you were there dressed as Santa."

The man shook his head. "I'm afraid you've mistaken me for someone else. Perhaps I have a double."

"Perhaps," Nick said suspiciously.

Right then, the doors opened. "This is me," Mr. Simonson said, nodding and waving a hand. "Good day to you all."

And as he stepped out, the four glanced through the doors to the office directory posted on the wall. Unlike most other floors in the building that held dozens of offices, this sign only displayed one name.

Simonson Toy Company.

Jeannie looked at Nick, then John, then Monica, all of them staring at each other but none of them willing to utter a word.

"Okay, so that was weird," Nick finally said. "Was it me, or did that guy look exactly like that whack nut Santa that was working our party?"

They all shrugged.

"I'd stake money on it," Nick insisted. "I don't know what game the guy was playing, but I never forget a face."

"Well," Jeannie said, hoping to save Nick from his misery. "Whoever it was, I'm glad the man was at our party. That night certainly changed *my* life for the better."

John Jr. nodded. "Mine, too."

"Yep," Monica agreed.

"Yeah, but that guy—I know that was him. And don't

you think it's strange that—" Nick started, but John cut him off.

"Nick," John said, clapping Nick on the back. "There are some things in life you just don't question." Then he pointed to the hallway as the doors came to a close. "That, my friend, is apparently one of them."

* * * * *

*See below for a sneak peek from our classic
Harlequin® Romance® line.*

Introducing DADDY BY CHRISTMAS by Patricia Thayer.

MIA caught sight of Jarrett when he walked into the open lobby. It was hard not to notice the man. In a charcoal business suit with a crisp white shirt and striped tie covered by a dark trench coat, he looked more Wall Street than small-town Colorado.

Mia couldn't blame him for keeping his distance. He was probably tired of taking care of her.

Besides, why would a man like Jarrett McKane be interested in her? Why would he want to take on a woman expecting a baby? Yet he'd done so many things for her. He'd been there when she'd needed him most. How could she not care about a man like that?

Heart pounding in her ears, she walked up behind him. Jarrett turned to face her. "Did you get enough sleep last night?"

"Yes, thanks to you," she said, wondering if he'd thought about their kiss. Her gaze went to his mouth, then she quickly glanced away. "And thank you for not bringing up my meltdown."

Jarrett couldn't stop looking at Mia. Blue was definitely her color, bringing out the richness of her eyes.

"What meltdown?" he said, trying hard to focus on what she was saying. "You were just exhausted from lack of sleep and worried about your baby."

He couldn't help remembering how, during the night, he'd kept going in to watch her sleep. How strange was that? "I hope you got enough rest."

She nodded. "Plenty. And you're a good neighbor for

coming to my rescue."

He tensed. Neighbor? *What neighbor kisses you like I did?* "That's me, just the full-service landlord," he said, trying to keep the sarcasm out of his voice. He started to leave, but she put her hand on his arm.

"Jarrett, what I meant was you went beyond helping me." Her eyes searched his face. "I've asked far too much of you."

"Did you hear me complain?"

She shook her head. "You should. I feel like I've taken advantage."

"Like I said, I haven't minded."

"And I'm grateful for everything…"

Grasping her hand on his arm, Jarrett leaned forward. The memory of last night's kiss had him aching for another. "I didn't do it for your gratitude, Mia."

Gorgeous tycoon Jarrett McKane has never believed in Christmas—but he can't help being drawn to soon-to-be-mom Mia Saunders! Christmases past were spent alone…and now Jarrett may just have a fairy-tale ending for all his Christmases future!

*Available December 2010,
only from Harlequin® Romance®.*

HREXP1210

HARLEQUIN®

A *Romance*

FOR EVERY MOOD™

Spotlight on

Classic

Quintessential, modern love stories
that are romance at its finest.

See the next page
to enjoy a sneak peek from
the Harlequin® Romance series.

Silhouette Desire

USA TODAY bestselling authors

MAUREEN CHILD

and

SANDRA HYATT

UNDER THE MILLIONAIRE'S MISTLETOE

Just when these leading men thought they had it all figured out, they quickly learn their hearts have made other plans. Two passionate stories about love, longing and the infinite possibilities of kissing under the mistletoe.

Available December wherever you buy books.

Always Powerful, Passionate and Provocative.

REQUEST YOUR FREE BOOKS!

2 FREE NOVELS
PLUS 2
FREE GIFTS!

HARLEQUIN®

Blaze™

Red-hot reads!

COMING NEXT MONTH

Available November 30, 2010